SPECIAL MESSAGE TO READERS

This book is published under the auspices of

THE ULVERSCROFT FOUNDATION

(registered charity No. 264873 UK)

Established in 1972 to provide funds for research, diagnosis and treatment of eye diseases. Examples of contributions made are: —

A new Children's Assessment Unit at Moorfield's Hospital, London.

•

Twin operating theatres at the Western Ophthalmic Hospital, London.

•

A Chair of Ophthalmology at the University of Leicester.

•

The establishment of a Royal Australian College of Ophthalmologists "Fellowship".

You can help further the work of the Foundation by making a donation or leaving a legacy. Every contribution, no matter how small, is received with gratitude. Please write for details to:

**THE ULVERSCROFT FOUNDATION,
The Green, Bradgate Road, Anstey,
Leicester LE7 7FU, England.
Telephone: (0116) 236 4325**

**In Australia write to:
THE ULVERSCROFT FOUNDATION,
c/o The Royal Australian College of
Ophthalmologists,
27, Commonwealth Street, Sydney,
N.S.W. 2010.**

I've travelled the world twice over,
Met the famous: saints and sinners,
Poets and artists, kings and queens,
Old stars and hopeful beginners,
I've been where no-one's been before,
Learned secrets from writers and cooks
All with one library ticket
To the wonderful world of books.

© JANICE JAMES.

CONSIDER THE LILIES

Kirsty Trensham's mother died when she was born and her father brought her up, but sadly he died when she was only sixteen. Kirsty then went to live at Refuge Farm, where she spent several happy years. When she eventually inherited the farm, Kirsty decided it would make an ideal holiday home for under-privileged city children. Her neighbour, Leif Amundsen, a tall, blond Norwegian, offered to help with the property alterations, but his sister-in-law, Leila Fennel, disliked Kirsty and set out to cause trouble.

MARJORIE WHITLEY

CONSIDER
THE LILIES

Complete and Unabridged

ULVERSCROFT
Leicester

First Large Print Edition
published June 1995

British Library CIP Data

Whitley, Marjorie
    Consider the lilies.—Large print ed.—
Ulverscroft large print series: general fiction
I. Title
813 [F]

ISBN 0–7089–3321–1

Published by
F. A. Thorpe (Publishing) Ltd.
Anstey, Leicestershire
Set by Words & Graphics Ltd.
Anstey, Leicestershire
Printed and bound in Great Britain by
T. J. Press (Padstow) Ltd., Padstow, Cornwall

This book is printed on acid-free paper

1

"MANAGE it? Me? No problem. It'll be a doddle!" Kirsty's confident words came back into her mind as she reached the crest of the hill and looked down on her new home. She had forgotten the mud, the black squelching mass constantly covering the yard on anything but the windiest or warmest sunny days. Today was neither.

The rain driving steadily throughout the entire journey, forming rivulets down the train windows and effectively blotting out the bleak March scenery, had ceased only in the last half-hour. Kirsty could still hear it dripping through the tall Wych Elms at the side of the road as she stood for a moment to catch her breath before making the descent.

Even now it seemed impossible that she was actually here, that at last there was a place which she could really call her own.

Her friend Sarah's scepticism was brushed aside. Typically, she laughed.

"Sarah, really! I can cope. There's got to be a funny side to every situation, and you can rely on me to find it. A sense of humour is all I'm going to need." Looking down on the place, doubts came creeping in for the first time since the solicitor had brought her the overwhelming news.

In one sense, she had been alone a long time. Since her father had died, sixteen years ago, she had been fiercely independent, masking her sensitive nature with a facade of cheerfulness. Yet she had never lacked company, or help when it was needed.

Could a twenty-six-year-old house-mother, straight from a city children's home, really cope alone with a fifty acre holding? A completely old-fashioned concern and, under the terms of the Will, to be run purely on conservationist lines, rather than economic.

Too right, she could! Kirsty's mouth curved upward and a sparkle came into her hazel eyes. If it meant trading that cramped, stuffy old room for a whole house and all the fresh air she could ever want, there was nothing she couldn't do.

Turning up the collar of her oilskin mac, and pulling the old sou'wester — both products of the last jumble sale — more firmly down over her chestnut hair, Kirsty marched forward eagerly. A few more yards and she would be putting her own key in the lock, stepping into her own kitchen.

As she approached the entrance, the sound of voices reached her. Her smile broadened. She had forgotten the hospitality of the country people. Neighbours would know that she had been travelling since the early hours, that she would be gasping for refreshment. Some of them were here to meet her. A welcoming committee, perhaps?

Perhaps not. As Kirsty put her small hand on the gate, the young woman in the yard bent down and stuck her head into the lower building attached to the house.

"This will have to come down to make way for . . . " The gate clicked. Pulling her head back, the woman straightened and turned towards the sound.

At five-feet-seven, with a slim yet softly rounded figure, Kirsty had never felt particularly small. Now she felt petite.

The man, clutching a clipboard of papers, must have stood at least six-feet. The woman was little smaller. A silver-tipped hand brushed a cobweb from her cropped, streaked hair as, straightening her expensive-looking camel coat, she glared at Kirsty.

"This is private property."

"True." Kirsty opened the gate. "And who might you be?"

"As far as this dreadful yard goes, we can . . . " The woman had turned back to what she was doing but, suddenly aware of Kirsty's approach, she turned back.

"Look, we're very busy here. What do you want?" The tone was curt and impatient.

"To begin with, I'd like to get to the door, if you . . . "

She broke off as, behind her, a vehicle screeched to a halt. The young woman's thin lips relaxed into a smile and, pushing past Kirsty, she rushed to re-open the gate.

"Leif! How nice. Come and tell me what you think."

Open-mouthed, Kirsty watched the door of the Range Rover slowly open and the tallest man she had ever seen issue forth. Mid-thirties, she judged, blond and bearded, he seemed to unfold — first the legs and then the body — the blue shirt straining against the buttons as he flexed muscular shoulders. He stretched his long arms above his head before relaxing to stand feet apart, thumbs hooked over the back of his belt, his piercing blue eyes raking the scene.

★ ★ ★

Reaching his side, the young woman slipped her arm into his, gazing up at him. "Naughty boy, you didn't tell me you were coming."

"You didn't tell me, either!"

Three pairs of eyes stared at Kirsty as she stood there, mouth twitching. She held up her hand. "I know. Don't tell me. This isn't Refuge Farm at all, is it? It's Lilliput. No, not Lilliput. That other place where Gulliver landed and all the people were big."

"Brobdingnag," supplied the bearded stranger. For a moment the brilliant blue eyes flicked over her, then he looked down at the girl holding his arm.

"What are you doing here, Leila?"

"That's the one." Kirsty grinned. "Brobdingnag. I always forget it. And that's the question I was about to ask. What are you doing here, Leila?"

The girl flushed an angry red, glaring at Kirsty.

"Miss Fennel to you — and would you kindly stop butting into other people's conversations? Who are you, anyway?"

Kirsty sauntered back to the gate.

"I thought you'd never ask. Kirsty Trensham. The new owner of Refuge Farm. So, if I'm not allowed to join in, would you mind taking your conversation elsewhere — and getting your lackey off my land?"

She pulled the gate wider, inclining her head towards the man with the clip board. Her mouth twitched again as he almost scuttled through and, deliberately, she beamed at all three in turn.

6

"Good morning all." She consulted her watch. "Goodness! Past lunchtime, and not a pot washed up. Must get on — lots to do." And with an airy wave of the hand, she swept across the yard, fishing the key from her pocket.

She was aware of them silently watching as she opened the door but, once inside, was so convulsed with laughter that, for a few moments, she saw nothing. Then, calming, she took stock of her surroundings. They came as something of a shock.

The bright cheerful room that she remembered looked damp and dismal. Limp, dingy curtains hung at the windows; patches of rust marked the formerly shiny black range. Tracks in the dust to a patch of chewed-up silver paper told their own story.

Slowly Kirsty made her way through the house. Dust, cobwebs, peeling paper — the pattern was the same in every room. She had known that the farm had been empty over the winter, while legalities connected with the disposal of the estate were settled, yet somehow she had not imagined it like this.

Coming out of the bedroom, she caught sight of her reflection in the mirror on the landing and screwed her small, slightly freckled features into a grimace.

Rubbing vigorously at a patch of mirror, she grinned into it, showing small white even teeth. "Say 'cheese'. This place is yours, remember, and it's beautiful — dust, cobwebs, mice and all!"

Tripping down the stairs, she removed the oilskin and sou'wester, hung them in the inner lobby, and danced into the kitchen. Standing in the middle of the floor, she surveyed the room with a determined air.

"Right, house, it's high time someone took you in hand. In a few hours, you won't know yourself."

But, a few hours later, her best friend Sarah might not have recognised Kirsty. Clad in a baggy pair of dungarees that had seen better days, a black woolly hat pulled down over her ears, covering every vestige of her thick hair, only the bright grin bore any resemblance to her normal self.

It was a grin of satisfaction. Dust and cobwebs had been cleared away, and a fire burned brightly in the shining black range, reflecting in the gleaming companion-set and horse brasses. The floor, stripped of old worn linoleum, had proved to be made of red hexagonal tiles, now scrubbed and sweet-smelling. The windows sparkled, and fresh curtains and cushion covers were put to air on a line attached to the high mantelshelf.

Taking a break, Kirsty sat in Albert Turner's high-backed wooden chair at the head of the scrubbed deal table. She could picture it surrounded by children's faces, one — her own — enthralled at his tales of nature and the living countryside around the farmhouse.

What a kind man he had been to invite mischevious city children to his home, she reflected.

With shame, she remembered her own misdemeanour, on her very first visit. Low lying as the farm was, tucked into a little plateau among steep, mostly wooded, hills, drainage was ever a problem, and water games definitely out.

One of the boys had unearthed a short

length of hosepipe and, fitting it to the yard tap, had seen fit to spray the girls as they came through the doorway. In a moment of fury, Kirsty grabbed the hose and turned it, with the intention of dousing the culprit. Instead, the stream, pressurised by her fingers, shot straight over the boy's ducked head and drenched a visitor, who was approaching the yard gate.

Kirsty could still see the startled expression on the young man's face, the dripping fair hair, the blue shirt turning almost navy as she dropped the hose and ran upstairs, sobbing. She could still remember being frog-marched outside and, looking up, after the red-faced stammered apology, to catch a momentary twinkle in the blue eyes of the stranger.

At least, after all these years, she seemed to be exonerated. What an honour to be selected, out of all the visiting children, to take over the farm. She intended to maintain the old standards to the best of her ability. And dreaming was not the way to do it, she affirmed.

Taking up the bread wrapper, she went to the door to tip out the last crumbs of her packed lunch for the birds. There had been a string of nuts and half a coconut-shell of fat put out when Kirsty had last visited. Soon the birds would enjoy those treats again.

As she closed the door, a sound came from further in the house a loud, insistent whining noise. Kirsty moved cautiously from room to room. What on earth could it be? This was one of the penalties of living alone for the first time. The sooner she got the place ship-shape, and ready to receive her own first batch of city children, the better.

She located the sound in the main bedroom. The sliding, small-paned, window was open just enough to allow the wind to whistle through the gap. Kirsty struggled, but was unable to move it and, after several attempts, decided to leave well alone.

Back downstairs, as she draped sheets and blankets over chairs by the fire, there came a sharp rap on the door.

11

She glanced round the room. She hadn't expected visitors so soon. Then, with a shrug, she opened the door. For a while, people would just have to take her as they found her.

Scraping mud from the sides of highly polished shoes was Robert Fawcett, Albert Turner's solicitor. He lifted the Homburg hat from his silver hair, and turned down the collar of his well-tailored black overcoat.

"Good afternoon, Miss . . . er . . . " He peered forward, regarding her closely. "Miss Trensham?"

Kirsty laughed. "Yes, it really is me under all this garb. My new image — do you like it?" She gave a mock curtsey.

He pursed his lips, frowning. "I must admit to a preference for your former image, Miss Trensham."

She laughed again and, pulling off the hat, she allowed her long curly hair to fall about her shoulders. "Come in, Mr. Fawcett, and do call me Kirsty."

He stepped inside, glancing round the room. "I do apologise for not meeting you. Miss . . . er . . . Kirsty. I understood that you were to come on a later train, and was appalled to find that you had walked from the station — on such a day, too."

Lifting the coffee pot from the top of the range, Kirsty smiled. "You forget that I spent a year with my father in the Amazon forests. A little English rain means nothing after that climate, as you can imagine."

The solicitor placed his briefcase on the table and began to sort through the papers. "I would think the English version somewhat colder and more uncomfortable. However, to business . . . "

★ ★ ★

Mr. Fawcett had come to ensure that Kirsty knew the boundaries of her property. It extended, as she thought, down to the river at the bottom and to the road on the west side, but the property to the east — which she had always known as Feversham's Copse — now went under the name of Fennel Farm Associates, owned by a certain Miss Leila Fennel.

Kirsty made a face, explaining the circumstances of her encounter with the lady that morning, and Mr. Fawcett smiled.

"I wouldn't worry too much. I'm quite sure that you'll get on splendidly, once they know you."

She sighed. "I expect so, but the attitude of the others was little better."

The solicitor looked up sharply. "There were others here?"

Kirsty nodded. "A tall, dark, full-faced man . . ."

"That would be Pratley, her foreman."

"And a huge, blond, bearded man."

"Leif Amundsen. Your neighbour from Tall Trees, over the road to the west. He has been manager there for a number of years, and approached us to purchase immediately following Mr. Turner's death. He was in fact, most anxious to take over both properties, until I informed him that Refuge was not for sale."

He snapped his briefcase shut, and Kirsty moved round the table.

"Leif, yes. I knew she called him by an unusual name."

Robert Fawcett nodded. "He's foreign. Danish, I think."

A bright smile came to Kirsty's face. "A Great Dane!"

He looked at her over his spectacles. "I hope you won't call him that to his face."

She laughed. "Don't worry. If there's any bad feeling between us it won't stem from my side."

★ ★ ★

The moment that Mr. Fawcett's car drew away, Kirsty swept her hair up under her hat, and took the bedclothes from the chairs. If she could get some degree of comfort into the bedroom, that would be enough work for one day.

The bedstead was brass, double-sized, the surface dulled by a grey bloom. The mattress felt extremely cold, if not damp. Kirsty made to lift it from the bed, and succeeded only in flopping on top of it.

So much for the saying 'as light as a feather', she thought, dragging it to the floor and tumbling it over and over, until she was able to send it rolling down the stairs to air by the fire.

Vigorous rubbing with a soft cloth soon

restored the bedstead to its former glory. She could do nothing yet about the damp, peeling wallpaper but, with the floor swept and the rugs shaken, clean curtains and dusted furniture, the room took on a cosier hue.

At last she was getting somewhere. Or was she? A few stairs up, struggling with the unwieldy mass of the mattress, Kirsty laughed at her own weakness. If she stood above it, attempting to pull, the mattress seemed to want to pull her down. If she remained below it, as fast as she persuaded one portion up a step, the remainder flopped back again. She was kneeling at the bottom, considering her next move, when another knock came on the door.

It was beginning to grow dark, and she had slid the bolts across on her last trip to the kitchen. Now she approached the door cautiously.

"Who is it?" Hand on the bolt, she waited, totally unprepared for the answer.

"Leif Amundsen."

Gripping the knob with her small fingers, she worked it up and down, struggling to draw the bolt back. When at last the door was open, she found that her neighbour was holding out a rope. "This is yours, I believe?"

She peered into the ever-darkening day. "What is it?"

A small smile flitted round his mouth. "A goat. A creature with four legs."

Kirsty let out a sharp breath. "Thank you. I know what a goat is. What I'm not so sure about is that it belongs to me."

He raised thick, blond eyebrows. "Of that I can assure you. Yours are the only goats around here."

"Goats?" Kirsty frowned. "You mean there's more than one?"

He nodded. "Undoubtedly."

Hazel eyes blinked. "Where? Oh, I'm sorry. In one of the outhouses, I suppose. I'd better go and see if anything else is in occupation."

He snorted. "I will go." He was already turning away. "Animals on the road in this light are an unnecessary hazard. I'm satisfied that they are safe if I check on the doors myself."

Kirsty stared after him. Mr. Fawcett was right about his nationality, it seemed — he pronounced 'w' as 'v'. Pity the

17

solicitor hadn't known enough of the man to warn her about his temper.

He was back in a moment. "The buildings are empty. I have put her in one of the loose boxes, and given her food and drink enough for tonight."

"You're very kind. Thank you very much."

"Animals need care." The blue eyes were frosty. "Do not forget her in the morning."

Kirsty bristled. "I won't. I would have seen to her sooner if I'd known she was there."

"Farms have often animals about." His tone was sarcastic. "I should have thought . . . "

★ ★ ★

He broke off as the loud whining noise sounded again. "You have a workman upstairs?"

"Just a wonky window," she said.

"There is something wrong?"

"It won't slide along," she explained, "so the wind is whistling through a narrow crack."

"I fix." Already he was tipping off rubber boots, and ducking his head to step in the door.

"Thank you, but I can . . . "

Her protest was in vain. He was en route for the stairs.

Kirsty left the door ajar, wondering what sort of man he was to come barging in on a woman alone. Had he really found a goat, or was it his intention to spy, since he had wanted the place himself? Or had he a yet worse motive?

As she moved cautiously in his wake, he turned quickly, catching her unawares. Kirsty stopped nervously. For a moment his eyes flicked over her face, then he said in a mock conspiritorial whisper, "You are completely safe. I like my women feminine."

"Do you now?" Kirsty moved forward briskly. "Then I must remember never to let you see me wearing my woman's weeds."

Reaching the bottom of the stairs, he looked from the mattress to Kirsty.

"Is it going up or down?"

Kirsty forgot her disgruntled feeling, and laughed. "It's a battle of wits. I

19

want it to go up, but it clearly wants to come down."

He gathered it together, swinging it on to one of his broad shoulders.

"It's a battle of strength, I think. Where . . . ?"

"In the bedroom." Edging round him, Kirsty pushed open the door. He dumped it on the bed, spreading it out evenly before looking up. "And that is the window?"

She nodded. "Yes, but I don't want to put you to any trouble."

"You wish it open, or closed?"

"Open, please, if you don't mind."

He slid it back halfway and turned, seeking her approval.

Coming up beside him, her head well below his shoulder, she took a deep breath of clean clear air. "That's lovely. Thank you."

"You like the fresh air?"

"Oh yes!" she said enthusiastically.

"Yet you live in the city." He looked amused.

"Not everyone that lives in the city does so by choice."

He looked down at her. "And not

every person that comes to live in the country is suited for that life, either."

"I shall manage." Hazel eyes flashed.

"You think so?" His piercing eyes moved from the mattress to the window.

"It's only the first evening, and already . . . "

Kirsty wheeled round to face him squarely. "Listen, I'm grateful for your help, but you must admit that I didn't ask for it, and you may rest assured that I will certainly not ask in the future."

The giant frame stiffened. "I might prefer that you did."

Kirsty stood her ground. "I'm sure you would — if only to prove that I can't manage on my own."

He opened his mouth to reply, then changed his mind and closed it again. For a moment he stood with his jaw clenched, breathing hard through his fine-shaped nose, glaring at her defiant face. Then silently he moved round her, and ran down the stairs three at a time.

Following more slowly, Kirsty watched the descent with amazement. The stairs were steep, with an exceptionally narrow tread. She would have expected such a

21

manoevre from a man of his height and frame to shake the whole house. Instead, his remarkable lightness of foot illustrated a high degree of physical fitness.

At the outside door he turned, straightening to his full height, only to double from the waist into a mock bow.

"Good night, Miss Trensham."

Kirsty inclined her head slightly, attempting a composure she did not feel. "Good night, Mr. Amundsen."

★ ★ ★

She was awake next morning by first light. Six-thirty saw a fire already burning brightly in the grate, and Kirsty on her knees rummaging in a cupboard for suitable clothing to inspect her domain.

The inclement weather, and her anxiety to achieve some degree of comfort before nightfall, had prevented any exploratory expeditions the previous day. Now she could contain her eagerness no longer.

Cheerfully, she donned the products of her search, laughing at the spectacle she presented in a voluminous duffle coat and size eight laced leather boots that she could almost turn round in.

As she pulled open the door, her smile of anticipation gave way to a gasp of astonishment. A whirl of snowflakes flew in, settling on her coat and the doormat, and blotting out her view of the yard. Kirsty hesitated only a moment, then she smiled, raised her chin and braved the elements.

The squelching mud of the day before had hardened with frost into deep ruts. She clumped and slithered over them, in the unaccustomed heavy boots, to the lower building which Leila Fennel had been inspecting when she arrived. The door was fastened with a large rusty iron sneck, but it swung so easily that she pitched forward landing in a heap across a bale of hay. It was lucky there had been no one there to see her, she thought with amusement.

A movement from the loose box reminded her that she was not entirely alone and, brushing the hay from her clothes, she crossed the concrete floor to inspect her livestock. The goat looked small, friendly, and somehow sympathetic.

23

"You won't tell on me, will you, Gertie? We women must stick together, you know."

As she spoke, the light from the doorway was suddenly blacked out. Kirsty turned, astonished, to find herself staring up at a stony-faced Leif Amundsen.

"Goodness me . . . " she blinked, "you're an early visitor. I wasn't expecting to receive anyone at this hour."

The narrowed eyes looked her up and down, taking in every detail of her odd assortment of clothing.

"Evidently. It's not early to me, of course. In these parts we are normally risen long before this hour, and on transportation days, such as this, our usual morning labours are already done."

"Big deal," said Kirsty, pulling a face.

His lips parted in disbelief. Clearly he had expected her to be embarrassed or intimidated by his scornful attitude; instead she was amused.

* * *

"What . . . " she raised her chin defiantly, "if I told you I was up at five?"

24

He tossed his blond head. "I would not believe you."

Grinning, Kirsty shifted her weight on to the foot nearest to him, and leaning forward, held up a finger. "And you'd be right — because I wasn't. And what is more I don't intend to be in the future. From now on not so much as half a toe will escape the bedclothes before I am good and ready. You see the name on the gate? Refuge Farm. That's what it says, and that's just what it is. One small corner of the world where all creatures, large and small, can live their lives without harrassment — including the owner."

She rocked back to stand squarely on both feet, folding her arms, eyes coolly appraising him.

"Now, having established that fact, to what do I owe the honour of this dawn visitation — presuming there is a reason other than to spy out my sleeping habits?"

He thrust forward a parcel. "Since I am passing the gate, I bring you the accounts."

Kirsty frowned. "Accounts?"

"It's a book for taking a note of expenditure," he said patiently.

Kirsty cut him short. "All right, I know what accounts are. I was just a little taken aback at the fact that they are in your possession, as opposed to being on my premises or in the hands of the solicitor."

Leif gave a curt nod. "I see. Since our two farms were run in conjunction during Mr. Turner's lifetime, the accounts for both were done at Tall Trees — my place. I have kept the books in order until your arrival."

Kirsty took the parcel from him. "I understand. Thank you." She hesitated, then decided to make a friendly gesture. "Would you like a cup of coffee?"

He shook his head. "No, thanks. Today I am very busy." He turned to go, motioning towards the loose box. "The goat will have to be milked."

Keeping a serious face, Kirsty clapped a hand to her head in mock anxiety. "So it will. I wonder if I can do it? Let me see, you pump its tail up and down, don't you?"

For a moment an expression of horror

26

mingled with disbelief registered on his face, then he saw her mouth twitch.

His blue eyes flashed. "The care of animals is not a laughing matter."

Kirsty smiled. "Oh, I don't know. I can find something to laugh at in every situation."

He snorted. "This I see. It's impossible to conduct a serious conversation."

She shrugged. "Women take things far less seriously than men — and I thought you liked women to be feminine?"

The tall Scandinavian raised his head arrogantly. "Feminine, yes, not flippant. I hope for the sake of the animals that your hands are more capable of dealing with practical matters than your head seems to be. God dag, Miss Trensham," he said, slipping into his native language.

Ducking his head, he stepped outside and strode off across the snowy yard. Kirsty's eyes twinkled as she watched the receding ram-rod back and stiff, jerky gait. The Great Dane was cross, convinced that Refuge Farm was in the hands of an incompetent, half-witted clown.

So many country people seemed to

labour under the impression that 'townies' had scarcely so much as seen a blade of grass in their lives, let alone had the knowledge to nurture one. This particular townie, however, could in all probability recognise the flora and fauna of more regions than many of the locals could pick out on the map — and as for the care of one small goat . . .

She turned her attention to her charge, now raised by her forefeet on a rock inside the loose box, peering through the rails. Kirsty had often helped with the goats during her visits to Refuge.

"Now, Gertie," Kirsty spoke aloud, inspecting the pen, "warm water, I think, this morning, and then we'll see if some of these sacks contain some concentrates to keep you occupied. I could be somewhat out of practice, so you'd best keep very still for both our sakes."

Kirsty's fears were unfounded. Her companion was the quietest of creatures, and Kirsty's small gentle hands had not lost their touch. Soon the last, creamiest part of the milk was frothing into the white enamel bucket, and she was ready to re-fill the hay rack with an armful of rough dried herbage.

"I wonder where your friends are, Gertie?" From the doorway, Kirsty took a last look back at the forlorn creature. Then her eyes swept the empty yard. "And mine, for that matter," she added.

Much as she had longed for this freedom, it would be nice to see a friendly uncritical face — instead of the haughty expression of Mr. Leif Amundsen, which would keep drifting into her mind.

She stepped out into the yard. The blizzard had abated, and small white clouds scudded across a clear blue sky. Kirsty felt suddenly ashamed. Her first day in this lovely place and already she was questioning her fate. Where was her spirit of adventure?

★ ★ ★

In the direction of the wood, a sparrowhawk arrested its flight, hung for a moment motionless in space, then dropped like a stone to the far side of the paddock, just before the trees.

It was one of the wild creatures in her

care. Gertie was not her only charge; there were others as yet unseen. Quickly Kirsty set the milk to cool in the stone sink, and banked up the fire. The boundaries needed checking constantly, and there was no time like the present. She could collect her luggage from the station later.

The ground was damp and soft in the shelter of the trees. Kirsty skirted a patch of snowdrops nestling at the foot of a tall sycamore, the delicate white petals just beginning to open. The first flowers: soon winter would give way to spring and the quiet woods would be alive with voices.

As she moved on, a speckled thrush, disturbed by her movements, flew across her path, dropping the threads of grass from its beak.

Next time she would be sure to have more suitable footwear. The laced leather boots could not be controlled enough for quiet movement. Every creature in the wood must be aware of her presence.

Reaching the river, Kirsty made her way along the bank towards the blackthorn hedge at the eastern side of her property, bordering what she had always known as Feversham's Copse — now owned by Leila Fennel.

Horrified, she stared over the top of the depleted thicket. Where were the tall Scots pine, the wych elms with their ruddy blossoms, the quivering aspen? Horizontal trunks and wood chips dotted about the clearings told their own story. Surely the indiscriminate cutting down of trees was frowned upon by every conservancy organisation in existence?

Sadly, she turned away, scarcely noticing the rustlings, and half-completed nests in the hedgerows, which would have been her delight on the way home.

Half-an-hour later, retracing her steps across the paddock, a few acorns and a single broken twig of hazel catkins clutched in her hands, the sight of the chopped trees was still with her. Had Refuge Farm fallen into the uncaring hands of Leila Fennel, such might have been the fate of her own woodland.

She stopped short, her mouth set in a determined line. It would never happen. Suddenly she was sure of her vocation. This land would be preserved in its natural form always. She would starve before she would allow it to be taken over by anyone who thought otherwise. The Trenshams were well known for sticking to their principals. The last of the line she may be — she would not prove to be the least.

Back in the yard, a small drift of unmarked snow caught her eye. On impulse, she stepped into it, placing one foot directly after the other to impress a single line, the start of the letter K.

"What are you doing?"

The voice, coming suddenly as Kirsty hopped from the top of the straight stroke to start the downward leg, startled her and she stumbled.

Regaining her balance, Kirsty stared at the eyes peering through the bars from the roadside of the main gate.

Moving towards them, she laughed. "Drawing the letter K. Are you coming in?"

At once the gate clicked open to reveal a small girl about five-years-old.

"Why 'K'?" Wide blue eyes stared straight into her own.

"It's the first letter of my name."

"Can I do mine?" The child moved nearer.

"Of course." Kirsty nodded. "What's your name?"

The girl smiled. "Minna. Is it a race?"

"No." Kirsty shook her head. "That wouldn't be fair because I've already started. Let's see if we can do a nice M, shall we?"

Holding Kirsty's hand for support, the child placed one tiny foot after the other, carefully forming the letter.

When she had finished, Kirsty clapped her hands. "That's very good, Minna. Shall I finish mine now?"

"Ja."

Kirsty's head jerked up and she regarded the girl more closely. Bright blue eyes, blonde hair peeping from under the woollen hat. This was Leif Amundsen's child. For a moment she was still, an unaccountable sense of shock running through her. She hadn't thought of him as a married man.

Then she shook herself. She had not thought of him at all. Husband and father — what did it matter? His wife was welcome to this arrogant man.

"What's the matter?" Puzzled innocent blue eyes stared up at her.

Quickly Kirsty pulled herself together. "Nothing, darling." She finished the letter and stepped back. "There."

"That's not right." Minna put her head on one side. "It's like this." She marked the snow out in a half-circle.

"Ah . . . " Kirsty smiled . . . "that's 'C' for cat. Kirsty is spelt with a 'K' like the one in . . . er . . . "

"Knife," supplied a bemused voice from the gateway.

She didn't need to look up to recognise the owner. "Thank you very much. You're a great help."

The gate clicked shut and Leif approached. "It's not my fault you have a stupid language."

Kirsty sighed, her eyes sliding from him to Minna, still waiting expectantly. "A word beginning with K . . . I know . . . kaleidoscope." She smiled at Minna triumphantly.

The child blinked, clearly uncomprehending.

"You don't know what a kaleidoscope is?"

Minna shook her head.

Kirsty crouched down, drawing with her finger in the snow.

"It's a toy. A long tube, like this . . . with mirrors fixed all down the inside. In the bottom of the tube are coloured bits — beads, plastic." She stabbed her finger into the snow, marking them out. "When you shake the tube and look through it, the mirrors show pretty patterns."

Minna smiled. "Have you got a kly . . . a kly . . . ?"

"Kaleidoscope," supplied Kirsty. "Yes, but it's still packed in my luggage. Perhaps you can come back another day?"

Minna ran to Leif, clasping her arms round his legs. "Can we, Farbror?"

Farbror. How lovingly the child spoke to her father.

Leif placed a huge hand gently on the bright head, smiling down at her. "Ja, but remember if you drop it the mirrors will break. You must be very careful."

Minna jumped up and down with excitement. "I promise, I promise."

Kirsty laughed, glancing at Leif. "Did

you come seeking me?"

He shook his head. "No. I come seeking Minna . . . " he bent nearer the child, his tone and expression suddenly stern . . . "who is not where she is supposed to be."

Minna's face puckered. "Why do I have to stay there? I don't like Miss Fennel."

Kirsty couldn't agree more. Her barely suppressed grin did not pass unnoticed. Leif glared from one to the other.

"It's not a question of like or dislike. Is simply a necessity for this morning. In future . . . " he looked directly at Minna . . . "you will do as I say. And you . . . " he turned to Kirsty . . . "will conceal your amusement and keep out of my affairs."

Kirsty made a face. "Don't worry, Mr. Amundsen. I'm not the sort of person to get mixed up in anyone else's . . . affairs."

His face flushed an angry red, and he drew in a sharp breath. For a moment it seemed that he would reply, but, even as his lips parted, he changed his mind and snatched the child's hand.

"Come on, Minna."

As the Range Rover disappeared from view, Kirsty ruefully punched the air with her fist. What was the matter with her? Why could she present a perfectly even-tempered appearance to all but those who mattered most?

She kicked savagely at the snow. Hadn't she told herself, only minutes ago, that Leif Amundsen's opinion mattered not at all? And wasn't that just as it should be?

The shrill call of the telephone prevented any further thought on the subject. The instrument was one of the few modern conveniences that Albert Turner had allowed himself; she was very glad of it.

So, apparently, was her friend and fellow housemother.

"Oh, Kirsty," the voice came as soon as the receiver was lifted.

"Trouble, Sarah?" Kirsty was quick to recognise the anxiety in her friend's tone. "What can I do?"

"Take Timothy Hurst for a while?" asked the other. "The situation is fairly desperate at the moment or I wouldn't be planting him on to you so soon. I realise you'll barely have unpacked."

Kirsty laughed. "I haven't. My luggage is still at the station." She paused, remembering the boy in question. "When did Timothy come back?"

"Today, would you believe? In the middle of all the turmoil, back comes his mother as usual, saying it's not convenient to have him at the moment." Sarah sighed. "We all knew it wouldn't last, of course, but today of all days!"

Kirsty was puzzled. "What's special about today?"

"The storm." Sarah sounded astonished. "Didn't you have a storm? Half the roof blown off and rain pouring in — and our new building only partially usable as yet. We're fitting in with a shoehorn now — there just isn't room for one extra. So we thought since he knows you . . . ?"

Kirsty laughed. "All right, Sarah. You've convinced me. When can I expect him?"

"This evening, about seven." Suddenly the voice was brisk. "If I hurry I can get him on the lunchtime train."

Replacing the receiver, Kirsty stood for a moment, taking stock of the situation.

38

It had always been her intention to take children, but not yet, not until the better weather came, and she was more settled.

Still, what did it matter? Timothy had nowhere to go, and she knew the feeling. He would be company and no doubt she would cope perfectly well. There was too much to do to brood — another bedroom to prepare, shopping to do and a nourishing meal instead of the quick sandwich that she intended to make for herself. At least she had inherited a rather battered pick-up with the farm, so transport would be no problem.

Setting to work with a will — airing bedclothes, sweeping and polishing — her mind remained elsewhere.

Timothy. Nine years old and with no one really to care; shunted backwards and forwards by his mother, who turned her affection on and off like a tap, according to the current man in her life. Little wonder that the boy was constantly in trouble. Perhaps in the country there would be more to occupy his mind. He might respond better to a one-to-one relationship. He might even be a help to have around, she thought hopefully.

Kirsty gave a wan smile. Who was she kidding? There was little doubt that they would totter from one disaster to the next, but life wouldn't be dull from now on, that was certain!

★ ★ ★

Seven o'clock saw steadily falling snow, and Kirsty on the station platform, anxiously jangling the pick-up keys in her hand. She was well aware that anything could have happened between Sarah putting Timothy on the train and him reaching his destination.

Her fears were not unfounded. When Timothy stepped on to the platform, he was not alone. A familiar expression of defiance on his pinched little face, his left arm was firmly in the grip of the train guard. On his right marched a woman.

Her attitude of outrage would have been enough to strike horror in Kirsty's heart had the woman been a stranger — hopefully never seen again after this incident. Unfortunately, she was not. The woman was Leila Fennel.

Framed in the doorway of the station office stood a porter and a burly policeman. Clearly, news of the incident — whatever it was — had been flashed on ahead.

"Name, young man?" The sergeant looked sternly at Timothy.

Timothy stood silent and belligerent.

"Timothy Hurst," supplied Kirsty. "He's come to stay with me."

"I might have known," Leila burst forth, "that you'd have a hand in this."

"If you don't mind, Miss . . . " The policeman quietly admonished, still closely watching Timothy. "I understand, my lad, that you were attempting to steal from this lady's bag?"

"I wasn't, neither." Timothy glared.

"I wasn't is sufficient," Kirsty corrected automatically.

The sergeant's eyes slid to her and back to the boy.

"What were you doing?"

"Not telling you." Timothy stuck his chin in the air.

Kirsty stepped forward. "Timothy . . . " her voice was quietly menacing . . . "you will tell us exactly what you were doing with Miss Fennel's bag, and you will tell us now. Right?"

The sudden sharpness of her tone made Timothy jump. He mumbled something unintelligible.

"Loud and clear, please, Timothy!"

At Kirsty's command, the boy spoke up grudgingly. "Wasn't taking nothing out. I was putting something in."

Kirsty swallowed, remembering past incidents. "What were you putting in, Timothy?"

He grinned. "Turnip."

Leila snorted, snatching at the fastening. "I don't believe you."

"Wait!" Kirsty put out a restraining hand. "I have a suspicion that when Timothy said 'Turnip' he was not referring to a harmless inanimate vegetable."

She turned to Timothy. "You weren't, were you?"

Eyes locked, Kirsty and the boy shook their heads slowly in unison.

"In fact it was something that slithers, crawls, jumps, or generally creeps about, which you have named 'Turnip'?"

Both heads nodded in perfect time.

"Does it bite?"

At Kirsty's question, Timothy looked scornful. "Nah!"

"No," corrected Kirsty. "What is it, then? You'd better tell us."

"S'only a toad." Hands in pockets, Timothy shrugged.

"A toad!" Leila shrieked, flinging the bag to the floor.

Kirsty retrieved it. "May I?"

Opening the bag, she slid her hand inside and brought forth the brown, wrinkled creature, its coppery bulbous eyes narrowed to a slit in the sudden bright light. She handed it to Timothy.

"Now keep hold of it — and apologise at once to Miss Fennel."

"Sorry, Miss Funnel."

Leila glared. The words came promptly, but the boy looked far from sorry. Kirsty was certain that the name had been mispronounced purposely.

A fast evacuation seemed to be called for. She glanced at the policeman.

"A boy's prank, surely? No harm done."

"No harm? No harm?" Leila's voice rose in a crescendo. "All my personal things tainted by that vile creature!"

"Perhaps you would check that there's nothing missing, Miss?" The placating voice of the sergeant broke into her protesting wail.

Grudgingly, Leila flicked through the handbag. "It all seems to be here."

"Then might it not be as well to let the young man go on his way — on the promise that he behaves himself in future?"

His face was serious, but there was a definite twinkle in the policeman's eye as he glanced at Kirsty.

In the face of their obvious agreement, Leila capitulated. She turned sharply, slamming out of the station.

Kirsty ushered Timothy into the pickup with all speed. The sooner she got the boy safely back to Refuge, the better.

★ ★ ★

In Rondale, especially in the shelter of the station buildings, the air seemed calm and the snowflakes floated gently down. On the open road it was a different story. The wind gusted with surprising strength, whirling the snow into blizzard conditions as Kirsty eased the pick-up slowly forward.

They had travelled some distance when a vehicle appeared behind them, clearly moving fast. It seemed only seconds before the lights were directly behind, dazzling Kirsty with the reflection in the mirror, as the driver attempted to pass.

Suddenly, with a burst of unexpected speed at the narrowest part of the road, the vehicle shot forward. For a fleeting moment, as both cabs were alongside, Kirsty recognised the smirking face of Leila Fennel, then the other vehicle cut directly across her path.

In a frantic attempt to avoid collision, Kirsty swerved to the left, mounting the snow-covered verge. For a few yards they bumped their way over the uneven surface, unable to move back on the road for the other vehicle, which was travelling — it seemed deliberately — only half a car length ahead.

She was easing her foot off the accelerator, in a bid to tuck in behind the Range Rover, when the grass verge suddenly petered out. Before she could take action, the nearside front wheel ran straight into a deep ditch.

Timothy wound down his window, sticking his head out to shout a few choice expletives as the Range Rover accelerated away.

"Timothy!" Kirsty was shocked. "That isn't going to help matters."

He glared. "Road hogs!"

"Make sure your seat belt is fastened. I'm going to attempt to reverse out," Kirsty said as calmly as she could.

Attempt she did, again and again, but it was clearly hopeless. The gully was too deep, and the snow too thick to get a grip. The wheel spun round on the spot, digging them ever deeper in.

"I'm sorry, Tim," Kirsty said with a sigh. "I'm afraid we're going to have to walk. In the morning I'll see if I can find someone who can pull it out."

Timothy shrugged. "Tractor'd do it, no sweat."

Kirsty laughed. "I don't doubt it. Unfortunately, I don't possess one."

"Ain't you got no neighbours what could lend you one?"

She made a face, overlooking the grammar. "Most probably, but that — she pointed after the fast-receding vehicle — was one of the neighbours, possibly two. It wouldn't surprise me in the least to find that The Great Dane was driving."

Timothy's sudden grin illustrated her mistake in allowing the name to slip. He made no comment, but she had little doubt that the information was being stored for future reference — to be aired at a most inconvenient and embarrassing moment.

Many a time on her father's expeditions, Kirsty had been glad to see their home base, but never more so than on this occasion. By the time they arrived, her fingers were so stiff with cold that she could scarcely unlatch the gate, and she had to apply both hands to the key to open the house door.

She poked the fire to a blaze, and they sat on the rug to eat their meal, revelling in the warmth seeping into their frozen limbs.

"Bed, young man," she commanded, as soon as they had finished. "What we both need now is a good night's sleep. I'll show you where to find everything, then I'll stuff our wet boots with paper so they'll be dry in the morning. And that is all I intend to do tonight!"

★ ★ ★

Unconcerned about the time of rising, and exhausted after the long walk home, Kirsty slept soundly and was surprised to wake early, feeling perfectly rested. She rose at once, singing softly as she worked, lighting the fire, washing up, setting the kettle and coffee pot on the range.

At seven-thirty, she donned duffle coat and boots and put up the fireguard. There was no sound from upstairs. With luck she would have Gertie milked before Timothy appeared, and they could breakfast together.

It was a beautiful morning. The air was still and sharp, a thick white frost sparkled on the tree by the gate and, high on the clear air, a skylark sang.

Kirsty's eyes shone. In spite of the snow, and the heavy leather boots, she felt like dancing to the stable. It was so good to be here.

"Hello, Gertie," she called out as she approached the loose box. "Here I am again. Have you been lone . . . "

She stopped, staring over the rails. In the loose box next to Gertie was another young goat — clearly in kid.

Kirsty grinned, delighted. "Hello, there! Where did you spring from?"

The note on the feed sacks did little to enlighten her: Your family has grown by one goatling, two guinea pigs, and 45 hens — 20 laying and 25 point of lay. Feed in respective sheds. Accounts attached. Will be in touch. J.C.

Kirsty tucked the paper in her pocket, puzzling over it. J.C.? The initials applied to none of the neighbours that she had met so far.

There was no address, no way of getting in touch for information on care of the stock. It would just have to remain guesswork until someone made an appearance and could be applied to for instruction.

The guinea pigs were friendly inquisitive creatures, coming forward to greet Kirsty, tipping up their dishes of chopped carrot and nuzzling her hand with their soft noses.

Smiling, Kirsty stroked their curly tortoiseshell coats. Abyssinians — they would appeal to Timothy and keep him out of mischief, with any luck.

Leaving them, she turned her attention to the goats.

"You shall be 'Gigi'," she told the new addition to her fold, as she changed her water and put fresh hay in the rack.

Aware that goats loved human company, Kirsty kept up a constant flow of conversation from the time she prepared the milking pen to washing the plastic armlets, which she used to cover the duffle coat sleeves. Later in the year the animals could be free to follow her about. For the moment, regular visits throughout the day would have to suffice.

Kirsty carried the milk back to the house and set it in the sink to cool. No sign of Timothy yet. Perhaps, if she located the hens, there might be eggs for breakfast.

The hen-hut stood in a piece of scrubland, next to the paddock, and to her delight, there were seven eggs in the nest-boxes.

She had filled the hoppers, and was carefully lifting the eggs into her bucket, when she was startled by a screech of car brakes. She made at once for the door but, as she pulled, someone on the outside pushed.

The door flew wide, both stumbled, and ended up in an ungainly heap on the floor, the crushed eggs beneath them.

"You are all right?"

The phrasing identified her visitor as Leif Amundsen. Gripping her elbows, he swung her to her feet.

Kirsty laughed up at him. "I was until you came."

Leif looked mortified. "I am so sorry. It's a disaster — and you laugh?"

She shook her head in reproof. "It's no disaster — just a minor mishap. Fancy scrambled eggs for breakfast?"

He crouched down, picking up the reasonably usable eggs and putting them into the bucket. "It's not funny."

★ ★ ★

51

Kirsty crouched down beside him. "It's not so terrible, either. You take things too seriously."

He looked directly into her eyes. "Life is serious."

"Not always." She hesitated. "Is there something wrong? Why did you come?"

He stood up, holding her elbow while she did the same.

"I come to see if you are all right?"

Kirsty looked blank.

"Your pick-up," he qualified. "It's yours, is it not? It's off the road."

"Ah." She nodded. "I see. Thank you for coming, but we are perfectly all right."

"We?" His forehead wrinkled in a slight frown.

"I have a visitor," she explained. "He isn't up yet. Would you like to come in for a coffee?"

He stepped back, raising a hand slightly. "I think not. Please forgive this intrusion."

Kirsty smiled. "It's no intrusion. It's very nice to know that someone is concerned about my welfare. However, if you really won't come in, you must excuse me hurrying away. If Master Timothy is awake, I shudder to think what mischief he's getting himself into."

Turning from closing the door, she caught an astonished expression on Leif's face.

"Your visitor is a child?"

"Of course, what did you . . . ?" Kirsty hesitated as realisation dawned. "Oh, I see, you were thinking that I had a lover ensconced on the premises? Well, I'm sorry to disappoint you, but I'm not that kind of girl! Very old-fashioned in this day and age, I know. I believe in love and marriage, and if I can't have that I'd rather have nothing."

She looked up to find him regarding her so seriously that she laughed.

"Sorry about the lecture. Are you sure you won't come in for a coffee?"

He smiled. "I think perhaps I will change my mind."

They found Timothy, still in pyjamas, staring up at the framed, embroidered sampler above the fireplace. As they came in, he turned.

"'Consider the Lilies'? It doesn't mean nothing, Miss."

"Call me Kirsty. It doesn't mean anything," she corrected. "But, yes, it does, as a matter of fact — it's a quotation from the Bible. 'Consider the lilies of the field, how they grow; they toil not, neither do they spin: And yet I say unto you, that even Solomon in all his glory was not arrayed like one of these'. Jesus was trying to explain to his disciples that, if they trusted in God, he would look after them just as he did the wild flowers."

Timothy looked puzzled. "I don't see why they would always wanting to be spinning round, anyway."

Kirsty smiled. "Not spin round. Spin thread, with a spinning wheel. It was simply an example illustrating that the wild flowers didn't have to work for their living, but they were still looked after."

"Oh, I see, Miss," he said gruffly.

"Upstairs now, Timothy, and get dressed."

Timothy departed, but was no sooner out of sight, than his head stuck back round the door. He looked straight at Leif. "You got a tractor?"

"Ja."

A grin spread over the boy's face, and he inclined his head towards Leif. "This is . . . "

"My other neighbour," Kirsty nodded hastily. "Mr. Amundsen . . . " she turned to Leif . . . "this is Timothy Hurst."

Leif smiled. "You need my tractor to pull out the pick-up, yes?"

Timothy raised his eyebrows at Kirsty. "Quick, ain't he?"

"Upstairs," Kirsty repeated in a threatening tone, and Timothy went.

Pulling out a chair, Leif sat down at the table. "He would like to come along, you think, in the tractor to collect your vehicle?"

Kirsty looked up from pouring the coffee.

"Oh, I don't know." She sounded doubtful.

Leif gave a rueful smile. "You do not trust me with the boy."

She shook her head. "It's not you I don't trust. There's children and there's Timothy Hurst."

"This I realise," he said with a wry smile.

They both laughed.

55

"I'm sure he'd like to go, if you think he won't be a nuisance," she told him. "You'll need me there, too, to drive the pick-up, won't you?"

Leif shook his head. "I'll take one of my men." He looked at his watch, then drained his cup. "It reminds me, I am on my way to pick up Harry. He insists on riding his bicycle in all seasons, and will not be pleased that I go, but on such roads he is not going to travel so uncomfortably to work for me. The coffee was good. Thank you."

At the doorway, he turned. "After I take Minna to school is a good time, yes?"

She nodded. "Yes. Thank you very much."

He waved a hand airily. "It's nothing."

Kirsty watched him go. How kind of him to turn back on the road to see if she was all right. How gentle his huge hands had been as he lifted her to her feet, and how sparkling his eyes, when . . .

How stupid to be carrying on like this! Kirsty brought her runaway thoughts to a sharp halt. What was she thinking of? A man with a wife and the sweetest little child — and not half an hour ago she was assuring him of her strict moral code.

A simple act of neighbourliness, and she was behaving like a love-sick teenager, dreaming about his hands and eyes, forgetful of all that had gone before. Only yesterday he had told her very clearly to keep out of his affairs: two days' acquaintance and her conduct had brought about a sharp reprimand, richly deserved. The man was a stranger — so why did it seem as if she had known him all her life?

Whatever the reason, Kirsty had no doubt as to her course of action. She would discourage any socialising between them. In any case, hadn't she more than enough to think about on her own doorstep?

In the first flash of excitement, she had rushed to accept her unexpected inheritance, convinced that her common sense and general good humour were all that was necessary to win the day. It was time now to get down to brass tacks, and examine the accounts.

While Timothy waited by the window, watching for Leif with the tractor, Kirsty sat down with a note-book and pencil. She scarcely noticed the boy hopping excitedly from one booted foot to the other, as she calmly made a list of their requirements.

Yesterday she had considered better-fitting working clothes for herself as the most urgent necessity. Now, after examination of Timothy's meagre wardrobe, warm clothes for the boy had taken pride of place.

Long after Timothy had gone, she was still poring over the books. When, at last, she put them away, one fact had become abundantly clear: Refuge Farm had been supported by regular injections of money from Tall Trees. The two had been run in conjunction — milk and eggs flowing one way, and hard cash the other — but even a child could see which place was not a viable proposition on its own.

"I'm off to talk to my goats," she decided. "I can't let myself get gloomy." She was still in the stable when Leif returned, driving her pick-up.

"Is Timothy in the tractor with the other man?" Looking past him into the yard, she noted at once that her neighbour was alone.

Leif shook his head. "No."

At his serious expression, Kirsty's eyes widened in alarm.

"Where is he?"

His eyes twinkled. "I leave him at the school. It's football on Fridays. The boy is good."

Kirsty nodded. "Yes, he is. I'd forgotten. Oh, but . . . " another thought struck her . . . "how will he get home?"

"I'll bring him with Minna, naturally."

"Thank you." She smiled. "And thank you for rescuing the pick-up."

He shrugged. "That's O.K." Then his eyes twinkled. "Now you can put the men's clothes back in the cupboard, yes?"

Kirsty smiled again, but said nothing. Much as she would have liked to put away her present clothing, it was as well that she could not. These working clothes were reasonably comfortable, and there were none as adequate in her suitcase. Besides, her desire for different attire was entirely based on presenting a more attractive appearance to this unfairly desirable, forbidden male.

The tractor rumbling to a halt prevented any further conversation. With a wave of his hand, Leif vaulted the gate and swung into the cab. Kirsty waved back, then turned at once and went into the stable. There was nothing to do in there, but she did not intend to stand watching him go.

"Start as you mean to go on," she told herself fiercely.

In spite of her resolution, when Timothy entered the house alone, and she realised that Leif and Minna had already gone on their way, she could not stem a small pang of disappointment.

A glance at Timothy put all such thoughts from her mind.

The toe of one boot was split, his trousers torn, the knuckles of his right hand were bleeding, and a deep blue line was already showing under one eye.

Kirsty turned him to the light for closer inspection. His jacket was soaked. Taking it by the collar, she peeled it off.

"What a state you're in! Have you been fighting again?"

Up went the chin in defiance. "They

called me a townie, Miss."

Kirsty laughed. "Well, so you are."

Timothy glared. "It don't mean to say I'm a wally. I reckon I could teach them a thing or two."

Kirsty reckoned he was right, though she doubted whether any of the mothers would want their sons to learn.

"The Great Dane stopped the fight, Miss! You should've seen. They was all on top of me and . . . "

"Were," interrupted Kirsty, "and you mustn't call him that."

" . . . and up he comes and lifts me right out of the middle, and into his tractor. It was like being beamed up into a spaceship."

"And did he say nothing about your clothes?"

"Nuffin at all, Miss. He's an ace bloke."

"Nothing," she corrected automatically, "and I don't suppose he cares. It isn't his responsibility to buy you new ones. We'll have to go shopping tomorrow, whatever the weather."

Since the village sported only one small general store, it was necessary to drive ten miles over the snowy roads into Malton.

Kirsty woke Timothy early, and by eight-thirty they were on their way, Timothy looking eagerly about him, Kirsty with her full concentration on driving. It would not do to slide into the ditch for the second time.

Her intention was to be back at Refuge Farm by lunchtime, and had it not been market day, and the town so busy, it might have been possible.

Having finally found a parking space, Kirsty was locking the door of the pick-up when Timothy pulled her arm.

"There's a Roman museum, Miss. Come on." He set off across the square.

Kirsty followed him up the steps. He did seem keen, and it might be a considerable time before they came here again. Once inside, examining the exhibits and discussing their uses with the boy, she became completely absorbed, all thought of haste forgotten.

"Just look at that child's boots."

The furtive whisper between two other visitors to the museum brought her back to reality. Hurrying Timothy out of the door, away from prying eyes, Kirsty was dismayed to find a snowstorm raging. She hastened to the cab of the pick-up.

Tucking her hair into the sou'wester, she held out the oilskin mac. "You put this on, Timothy. It's big, but it will keep you dry . . . "

She turned. Drat the boy, where was he?

Straightening, she spied him ahead, turning somersaults over the snow-covered railing bordering the car park.

"Timothy, be careful!" Her warning came too late. Even as she spoke, he slipped from the rail and fell flat on his back on the snowy pavement. He made no move to get up.

Kirsty rushed forward. He was so still. Unconscious? Spinal injuries?

Frantically, she slithered over the slippery ground, her eyes fixed on the motionless child. "Timothy! Timothy, love."

"Ha, ha!" As Kirsty reached the inert body, he suddenly sprang to life, pointing at her. "Had you going there, didn't I, Miss? Did you think I was a goner?"

Kirsty managed a weak smile. "Yes, I

did for a minute. Come on, now, there's a good boy. We have a lot of things to buy, and a limited time to do it in."

She moved off, proceeding down the walkway by the side of the church, expecting him to follow.

"Miss!" The boy's call went unheeded.

"Do come on, Timothy." Kirsty was fast losing patience.

"But, Miss . . . Look over there . . . It's the Great Dane!"

Kirsty wheeled round, wishing the ground would open and swallow her up. Timothy's tones were loud and clear and, as she followed the direction of his outstretched arm, she saw Leif hesitate in the doorway of the creeper-covered coffee shop across the road. His face unusually flushed, he was glaring directly at Timothy.

Unabashed, the boy grinned and waved. Slowly Leif turned his head, closely examining the whole of the area from the church to the cafe on the opposite corner. When his eyes finally came back to rest on the boy, he raised a hand in brief acknowledgement, before quickly ducking his head and disappearing through the doorway. Clearly he felt insulted, and would apportion the blame in the right quarter.

The shopping expedition was neither as brief or successful as Kirsty had hoped. By the time she had located the animal feed shop to pay the account, and bought strong school shoes and rubber boots for Timothy, a third of her bank account, half the money in her purse, and all the morning, had gone — and she had still done nothing about the boy's coat and trousers.

In the end it was due indirectly to Timothy's indiscretion that she found what she was looking for. Idly glancing along the road, while Timothy gazed spellbound into a toyshop window, she caught sight of Leif approaching, with Leila Fennel on his arm.

Heads down against the driving snow, they hadn't seen Kirsty and, grabbing Timothy's arm, she propelled him into a side street to find herself outside a charity shop. Without a second thought, she pushed open the door.

★ ★ ★

It was late afternoon when they returned home. The snow had sharpened into a deep frost, making the roads much more treacherous than on the ouward journey, and Kirsty breathed a sigh of relief as she parked the pick-up under the open barn.

An hour later, the stock fed and the milk cooling in the sink, Timothy came to stand by Kirsty, as she knelt trying to coax the fire into life.

"But what are we going to do, Miss?"

Kirsty laughed. "No wonder they called you a townie. There's no need to be bored in the country. I shall keep you so busy that you'll be glad to go to school on Monday for a rest!"

Whilst that statement was not strictly true, there was no doubt that Kirsty managed to keep the boy occupied, from the moment that he appeared downstairs the next morning, to the time he went to bed.

Together they made a nest of straw and leaves in a hollow in the stable wall for Timothy's toad, explored the wood, built a snowman, and finally had a snowball fight in the yard.

After spending most of the day in the crisp fresh air, Kirsty found herself unusually tired. Altering the parka and trousers that she had purchased for Timothy in the charity shop, she was hard pressed to keep her eyes open and, the moment she had finished, decided to call it a day.

Tumbling at last into bed, she was startled by the sound of the telephone. She glanced at the luminous hands of her bedside clock. Ten-thirty. Who would be ringing at this time?

Wearily she plodded downstairs and lifted the receiver.

"Kirsty Trensham."

"The boy goes to school tomorrow?" The question came with no preliminaries, the tone clipped and curt.

"Yes . . . yes, he does." She had already contacted the headmaster to make the arrangements.

"He may travel in my vehicle. It's stupid for us both to cover the same ground. Have him ready by half-past eight, please."

Kirsty blinked. "This really is very good of you, I . . . "

"Eight-thirty." There was a sharp click, and his voice was replaced by the dialling tone.

Kirsty was filled with remorse. What a good man he was. Despite her insulting name for him, he could still find it in his heart to help her. She must apologise at the first opportunity.

Her chance came the following afternoon. The sight of the snowman, as she turned from the stable door, had led her to wonder how Timothy was getting along at school. He had run off eagerly that morning, scrambling into the back of the Range Rover without a backward glance, while Leif sat, stony faced, staring straight ahead.

An apology was impossible while the children were present. She was wondering what to do, when it suddenly occurred to her that no mention had been made of Timothy's return journey.

It was not safe to take it for granted that her neighbour intended to collect both children, nor was it sensible to brave the roads herself, only to find that he had covered the same ground.

Nervously, she dialled the number listed under 'Tall Trees' in Albert Turner's notebook. There was a sudden click as the receiver was lifted.

"Leif Amundsen."

"It's Kirsty . . . Kirsty Trensham. I was wondering about the children coming home from school. Would you like me to go and . . . ?"

"I shall collect both children, naturally."

In spite of the coldness of his tone, Kirsty breathed a sigh of relief. "Oh, thank you. Thank you very much, Mr. Amundsen. I wasn't looking forward to the journey, I must admit."

"It's formal address, I notice, now that I do you a favour."

"Pardon?" Kirsty frowned, taken aback.

"Yesterday I am a foreign cur. I have a dog's name, ja?"

"No!" Kirsty protested strongly. "That's not how it was meant, at all."

"So how was it meant?"

"It was just a stupid joke. I didn't intend . . . "

"Exactly." He cut her short. "A joke. You laugh at me with the boy, and I am not supposed to know."

"That's not true!" Kirsty struggled to explain. "I don't laugh at people — except, perhaps myself. It was simply your tall stature and nationality that brought the name to mind, and that's all that was meant. It was stupid, particularly to let it slip in front of Timothy, and I am sorry."

"It's also incorrect." There seemed to be a slight thaw in his attitude.

"Incorrect?" Kirsty was puzzled.

"You think I am Dansk. It's not true. I am Norsk."

Kirsty grinned. She could almost see the proud tilt of the head. "Oh, I see. Norwegian is much better than Danish, I suppose?"

He allowed a small chuckle to escape. "Ja!"

She laughed. "I have an idea. If you are bent on Viking revenge, why don't you devise a name for me?"

"I have a name."

Kirsty was intrigued. "What is it?"

"I do not say."

Her grin returned. "Why, won't I like it?"

"I do not know."

"But you're not prepared to risk it." She clicked her tongue in disapproval. "Your ancestors were conquerors. They wouldn't have been afraid to say."

He was indignant. "Who says I am afraid? I do not wish to say."

Kirsty laughed. "Come on, I won't be offended, I promise you."

"My Viking ancestors would not have been persuaded by a woman."

"Depends how attractive she was, and what she was asking them to do."

Her quick rejoinder brought an immediate response. "If she has a sensual appearance, perhaps . . . "

She laughed, looking down at herself. "My present attire does little in that direction, I'm afraid, but perhaps we'd better not go into that. Now, what time can I expect young Timothy to descend upon me?"

"I deliver him to you around four o'clock."

"Thank you." She smiled. "Thank you very much."

It was good to be on friendly terms again. She determined that in future she

71

would go out of her way to extend the hand of friendship to the Amundsens, and any other neighbour that she had yet to meet.

★ ★ ★

All too soon, her resolution in that direction was stretched to the limit. Gradually she had settled into a routine, and found herself able to manage both the stock and the child with ease.

As the weeks passed, there remained just two problems unsolved — the extreme shortage of ready cash, and the impending birth of Gigi's kid.

The former would be resolved with the advent of better road conditions. Cheques for Timothy's board were now coming through with regularity, but it necessitated a trip to Malton to change them.

The latter was the more worrying. When Kirsty had been in residence a month, the mysterious 'J.C.' who had been in charge of the stock until her arrival, had still not come forward.

She toyed with the idea of approaching

Leif Amundsen, but dismissed it as bad policy. He already considered her to be an irresponsible clown. How much more would he be convinced if she admitted that she had not yet been in touch with the temporary goatherd, to make sure that feeding and management had been consistent? Having reasoned thus, it was all the more annoying that he should be present to witness the meeting when it finally came.

Her anxiety about the imminent birth was such that she was prompted to call the local vet. To Kirsty's surprise, her request that he call when in the area, just to look the animals over, resulted in a visit that very afternoon, and it was a very relieved and gratified young woman who repaired to the kitchen for a celebratory cup of coffee after the expert's departure.

He had expressed nothing but praise for her management, finding the animals in good condition, their quarters clean, and their diet more than adequate. Regarding her concern for Gigi, he allayed her fears at once.

"In all the years I have been in

practice," he told her, "I have known only one kid lost through a difficult delivery. Goats have a way of looking after themselves. Don't hesitate to call me if there are any problems, but I am extremely doubtful that there will be."

As soon as the weather showed signs of improvement, Kirsty grasped the opportunity to take the goats with her on walkabout, while she attended to her other duties outside. Soon they were following her like two dogs, nuzzling her sleeves and pushing their heads under her hand, craving affection. Given a sporting chance, they would have been in the kitchen, and would stand, feet on the stones and chins resting on the rails, bleating pitifully after her, as she disappeared through the stable door.

So it happened one afternoon in April. The bright crisp weather had given way once again to rain, which poured unceasingly from the heavens, turning the yard into a sea of mud under Kirsty's feet as she battled against a near gale force wind, to feed her hungry flock.

There being no possibility of taking the goats out, she attended to the hens first, and it was after Timothy's departure in the Range Rover that she opened the stable door to a sight that made her clap her hands in sheer delight.

"Gigi, you clever girl!"

In her usual pen, Gertie was peering through the rails at her companion, who stood calmly eating hay from the rack while, beside her, two almost-dry kids were already preparing to suckle.

Kirsty could not tear her eyes away from the perfect little creatures. Long after her outside jobs were done, she stood in the next pen, her arm round Gertie's neck, as fascinated by the new mother and her youngsters as the animals themselves.

It was past ten o'clock when she finally left them, reluctantly plodding back to the house to face the daunting task of scrubbing the laundry in the kitchen sink. Being accustomed to all the labour-saving devices in the children's home, it was a necessity to which she had not yet become reconciled, and it was only the safe arrival of Gigi's offspring which kept her from utter despair as, wringing the clothes with her bare hands, she found tear after tear in the clothes belonging to Timothy.

So it was an unusually dispirited Kirsty who shut the stable door on the bleating goats, early that afternoon, and turned wearily away — just as the well-known Range Rover pulled up at the gate.

As she expected, the man who emerged was Leif Amundsen. The woman, a stranger, seemed almost as huge. An old floppy hat pulled down over her eyes, and a black muddy mackintosh covering her ample proportions, she clicked open the gate and, in spite of a heavily plastered left leg, and cumbersome crutches, advanced on Kirsty at an alarming rate.

With some trepidation, Kirsty forced a smile. "Oh dear, what have you been doing?"

"What have you been doing, that's more to the point?" The woman's eyes blazed. "Those animals were in perfect condition when they left my hands — now listen to them!" She half-turned to Leif, who stood behind her. "I told you to leave them with me. Dressing to look the part is one thing — doing the job properly is another. Out of my way, young woman, while I see to the poor creatures!"

As the woman attempted to brush her aside, Kirsty planted herself firmly in front of the stable door, and folded her arms.

The woman snorted. "Oh, we've got something to say for ourselves, have we?"

Kirsty took a deep breath, trying to calm her rising temper, and deliberately smiled. "Yes, quite a lot, actually. Firstly, I don't dress like this out of a desire to emulate a farmer's boy. It is a simple matter of expedience. Regarding the other matter, your note clearly says . . . " She fished in her pocket, spread out the crumpled paper, and read, "I will be in touch shortly."

Glaring up at the woman, she thrust the note towards her.

"Since you gave no address or telephone number, I was forced to wait, hoping that you were as good as your word. When you proved not to be, I called in the vet, who was highly satisfied with my management. However, I'm sure you would like the chance to fault it somewhere, so if you would care to look around . . . ?"

★ ★ ★

Kirsty stood rubbing the nose of one of the guinea pigs through the wire netting, watching both pairs of eyes as they scrutinised spotless utensils, scrubbed-out milking stall, and fresh bedding.

In spite of her bravado, her heart was in her mouth as, finally, the woman turned towards her.

"Well done, young woman! I'm proud of you." She stuck out a broad hand. "Jenny Carter. Call me Jenny."

Kirsty was so taken aback that, gripping the hand, she laughed aloud with relief. "Kirsty Trensham. How do you do? Thank you very much."

Jenny pressed her lips together, and nodded, her eyes twinkling.

"Don't mind old Jenny. Bark's worse than her bite. What do you plan to do with the kids — bottle feed?"

Kirsty sighed. "I'd like to but, as you see, I've no spare pen and no feeding equipment. Besides, to be honest, I don't

78

know if I could take them away from her when it came to the crunch."

"Jenny has everything for feeding at Westfield." Leif spoke up for the first time. "It is a matter of you parting from the goat and her little ones — not so easy, I fear."

Kirsty looked sorrowfully at the little family. "I suppose it would be better for them — weaning later is such a painful business — but bottle feeding is so time consuming, and I couldn't pay."

"Bless you, love, I don't want your money." Jenny spoke briskly. "I love goats, and there's little else I can do with this gammy leg."

"But you can't do it all for nothing," Kirsty protested. "You'll have to provide feed and bedding and . . . "

"I'll send you one of mine," Jenny broke in, "then I can look after . . . what do you call her?"

"Gigi," put in Kirsty.

"That's it. I'll look after your Gigi and family, and you can look after my Mabel. We'll see how you get along with her."

Kirsty stared. "Mabel? But . . . " She frowned at Leif. "You told me that mine were the only goats around here."

"I did?" He looked more guilty than puzzled.

Her eyes narrowed. "You know very well you did. On the first day I came, when you found Gertie wandering in the road."

A low chuckle from Jenny made her turn her head sharply. She looked from one to the other.

"You didn't find her wandering at all," she accused. "You picked her up from Jenny and brought her straight over to me, didn't you?"

"I . . . er . . . " As Leif hedged, a faint sound caught Kirsty's ears.

"There's the telephone." She smiled. "Saved by the bell, but not for long. When I return I shall expect a full explanation of your conduct — and no conferring, mind!" She turned away — then, still moving off, half-turned back. "Better still, come in for a coffee so I can keep an eye on you!"

"Sorry about the clothes dripping everywhere," she apologised, as they moved into the house. "I've nowhere else to get them dry."

She picked up the telephone. "Kirsty Trensham."

"I'm so sorry to trouble you. I'm trying to locate Mr. Amundsen. Does he happen to be with you?"

The woman's voice sounded anxious. Mrs. Amundsen, perhaps? Did she often have to ring round to find her husband?

"Yes. Yes, he does, as a matter of fact," Kirsty struggled to cover her confusion. "Would you hold on a moment?" She held out the receiver, yet did not cover it, making sure that the caller could hear, as she said, "Mr. Amundsen, it's a call for you."

Leif came forward with a puzzled frown. "Thanks."

Reaching for the coffee pot, Kirsty was suddenly aware of a movement across the room and, looking up, found that Leif had raised his hand, indicating that she should wait.

His face was ashen. "Of course. It's best that I say nothing for the moment." He spoke in a low, urgent tone. "But I must go now."

Replacing the receiver, he turned to Kirsty. "I'm very sorry, but we are not

81

able to stay for the coffee. I must leave you." He looked from Kirsty to Jenny. "If you have decided to change over the goats, I can arrange transport for you. Forgive me, but now there is no time."

"Not to worry." Picking up her crutches, Jenny patted his arm and winked at Kirsty. "We can come again, can't we?"

Kirsty smiled. "Please do."

Jenny nodded. "What about Friday, then, for the goats? Kids'll be four days old then." She moved towards the door.

Kirsty followed, and leaned round her to open it. "Fine." She glanced at Leif. "I'll see you then, perhaps?"

He shrugged, and his blue eyes seemed suddenly full of sadness.

"Perhaps me — perhaps one of my men — but I shall arrange it for you."

They had reached the Range Rover when Leif suddenly turned back to Kirsty. "I'm sorry to ask at such short notice, but I may not arrive back in time to collect the children. Do you think that you could . . . ?"

Kirsty nodded. "Of course. Don't worry about that. I'll pick up Minna with Timothy and take her home. There will be someone there?"

He gave a small, tired smile. "Yes. Thank you."

Whilst it was clear that something had come up of a serious nature, Kirsty could not help feeling pleased to have an excuse to visit Tall Trees. She was eager, not only to see the home, but also the wife of the handsome Norwegian. If she could make a friend of the woman, it would surely weaken her desire to know more of the man.

Miraculously, the rain stopped shortly after lunch. The wind dropped, and Kirsty was able to change into what she called 'reasonable' clothes, for the trip. For the first time since her arrival, she wore a dress, and the blue of her coat accentuated the colour of her chestnut hair.

★ ★ ★

After collecting the children from school, it took but ten minutes to cover the familiar part of the route. Past the gate of Refuge Farm, the road continued to drop away, and soon they were at the lowest point, crossing the stone bridge over the swollen swift-flowing river.

Kirsty slowed the pace, gazing with admiration at the lofty trees rising on either side of the tarmac road, as it wound upwards towards Leif Amundsen's appropriately-named home.

The belt of Norway Spruce and Scots pine on the river bank gave way to roughly a mile stretch of mixed broad-leaved forest: stately oak, beech and ash, standing proud of small groups of coppiced hazel — each species at different stages of development.

Kirsty soon found herself in awe at the grandeur and vastness of it all, and by the time the road led her through the massive stone arch to the timber-built house beyond, she felt like dropping Minna outside, and turning tail.

Though the whine of a saw-mill, just visible through another belt of trees, proved it to be a hard-working establishment, this was no lumberjack's cabin, no forester's hut. It was a mansion.

Curved stone steps led up to a

full-length veranda, the fine matched woods complimented by the profusion of blossoms on the winter jasmine, covering half its length. Huge bay windows looked out on to purple heather in a perfect setting against pine and silver birch and, among the trees, patches of golden daffodils stirred gently in the soft breeze.

Leaving Timothy in the pick-up, Kirsty took Minna's hand and made for the steps. If she had known that Tall Trees was as luxurious as this, she would not have dared to come. Living among all this beauty, what must Leif think of Refuge Farm, with its peeling paint and muddy yard?

As they stepped into the veranda, the door opened and a plump, grey-haired woman bustled forward. Beaming, she held out both hands in welcome. "There you are, my dears. Come in, come in, all of you. The tea is all ready."

Kirsty blinked. "Oh, but I wasn't expecting tea."

The woman laughed. "I'm sure you weren't, my dear, but you are going to stay all the same." She looked round.

"Where's the little boy?"

"He's in the pick-up," said Kirsty, indicating with her hand.

The woman leaned round her, beckoning to Timothy, who climbed from the pick-up and came slowly forward, eyes wide in admiration at the scene about him.

"That's right. Now come along in, my dears. Off with your coats."

She led them through a spacious carpeted hall, past a wide sweeping staircase, to a huge pine-fitted kitchen.

"Now," she said, ushering them towards a large, well-laden table, "I'm Robbie. Moira Robertson, actually, but I became Robbie when I first went to the family over thirty years ago, and that I remained with our young lady here." She nodded towards Minna, then turned back to Kirsty, her eyes twinkling. "I'm so glad to meet you after all this time, my dear. I've been wondering why Mr. Leif looks for excuses to call at Refuge Farm."

Kirsty blushed. What an awkward remark to make, especially in front of his daughter.

"I'm afraid Mr. Amundsen thinks I am very inefficient, and is concerned

86

for the welfare of the animals. In fact, I manage well enough, for a novice," she said hesitantly.

"I am sure you do." Robbie patted her hand. "And you must not allow him to intimidate you, my dear. He's strong willed, but loyal and kind — and so gentle with the little one. It's such a pity . . . "

Her voice ended in a sigh, and there was a moment's silence. Then she smiled suddenly. "But come along, now, help yourselves. I know that little boys are always hungry."

Timothy proved to be no exception. Sandwich after sandwich, cake after cake, followed each other in such quick succession that Kirsty began to feel acutely embarrassed.

Watching him, she shifted uncomfortably.

Robbie laughed. "You have not seen Mr. Leif eat, my dear. It would take more than this to fill him." She turned to Minna. "What do we call these open sandwiches in Norway, Minna?"

Minna peeped shyly over her glass of fruit juice. "We call them smorbrod."

Robbie nodded. "Good girl. Mr. Leif

likes her to keep up her Norwegian, so that she is able to converse with her grandparents when they go to visit," she confided to Kirsty.

When Timothy had eaten his fill, Minna dragged him away upstairs to see her rocking horse.

"Min farbror made it for me," she told him, proudly.

Robbie smiled fondly after her. "She worships Mr. Leif."

Kirsty nodded. "I know. I had hoped to meet Mrs. Amundsen today. Can you tell me when she might be at home?"

"Fru Amundsen is in Norway, my dear." Crossing to the stove, Robbie took up the coffee pot to refill her own and Kirsty's cups. "I've heard nothing of an impending visit. Has Mr. Leif mentioned the possibility?"

Kirsty laughed, shaking her head. "I think we're talking at cross purposes. I meant Mrs. Amundsen junior, of course."

Robbie studied her for a moment with a puzzled frown.

"There is no Mrs. Amundsen junior, my dear. Mr. Leif is not a married man.

He has never been married."

"Oh." Kirsty was completely taken aback. "But I thought . . . " To her extreme annoyance, as her voice faded, she blushed.

The sound of children's laughter came from upstairs and, as Kirsty's eyes were drawn towards the open doorway, Robbie's face cleared.

"Of course. You thought because of the child . . . " She replaced the pot and came back to Kirsty, lowering her voice. "You see, my dear, Minna lives here with us because her mother . . . " She hesitated. About to sit down, she had brushed a napkin from the table, and bent to retrieve it.

"Because her mother . . . " she repeated, then stopped again, raising her hand to her suddenly ashen face. "Oh, my dear. I'm so sorry. I do feel so peculiar."

Too late, Kirsty dived for the hot water jug at the edge of the table. One moment she was waiting anxiously, intent on the situation about to be revealed; the next, she was staring in horror as the housekeeper lay unconscious on the floor among broken pieces of stoneware, and pools of steaming liquid.

The sound of running feet approaching down the stairs spurred Kirsty into action.

"It's all right, children," she called. "Robbie dropped the hot water jug. Back you go and play for five minutes, while we clear it up."

To her relief, the footsteps retreated. Snatching a towel, Kirsty thrust it under the cold tap and rushed back to the still form on the floor.

It seemed like hours before Robbie stirred and her eyelids flickered. Dabbing the cool water on her forehead, Kirsty was so thankful to see the first sign of life that she could have wept.

For a moment, the eyes blinked uncomprehending into her own, then an expression of profound chagrin came over the housekeeper's face.

"Oh, my dear," she murmured. "How dreadful of me. I'm so very sorry. Usually I manage to sit down before that happens."

Kirsty frowned. "Usually? It happens often?"

Robbie inclined her head very slightly in confirmation. Unfastening a cushion from one of the pine chairs, Kirsty slipped it under her head.

"Does Mr. Amundsen know?"

The older woman closed her eyes wearily, then opened them again. "How could I worry Mr. Leif with trivialities at such a time?"

The situation remaining unexplained, Kirsty could not fully agree with the remark. She eyed the older woman keenly. "It's not such a triviality any more, is it? Suppose it had happened when you were alone with Minna?"

Robbie sighed. "You are quite right, my dear. I suppose I should see a doctor."

"I think it would be best," Kirsty agreed gently, "and I think it should be now, while I'm here. I'll ring him, if you'll tell me where the telephone is."

★ ★ ★

The beautiful inlaid pendulum clock was just striking five-thirty as the doctor came down to the hall where Kirsty anxiously awaited his diagnosis.

Half-expecting the master of the house to come home at any moment, she felt shy and awkward, and wanted to be away. No doubt it had been Robbie's own idea to invite them to a meal; he would have no prior knowledge of it. That being the case, he would certainly not be pleased to arrive home, tired and hungry, to find the meal devoured and Kirsty in charge of his household.

She eyed the doctor apprehensively as he removed his glasses and tucked them into his top pocket.

"I would be happier to see Miss Robertson in hospital overnight," he sighed. "However, she tells me that Mr. Amundsen is not due to return until mid-day tomorrow, so there would be no one to look after the child."

Kirsty shrugged. "That's no problem. I can keep Minna with me."

"Are you sure?"

She laughed at his doubtful expression. "I'm certain. I was housemother to twelve in the children's home where I worked. I can certainly manage two. I'll reassure Miss Robertson, shall I?"

He smiled. "If you would be so kind. Meanwhile I can arrange a bed."

Although Robbie was a better colour than when Kirsty left her, she was clearly feeling far from well. Kirsty waved aside her protests.

"Minna is coming to stay with me. Now what would Mr. Amundsen like to eat when he comes home? What about . . . *lapskaus*, perhaps, with *flatbrod*?"

Robbie blinked in surprise. "A Norwegian dish? It would certainly please him, my dear, but can you really manage it?"

Kirsty laughed. "I can, as a matter of fact. I'm more capable that I look — especially when it comes to unusual accomplishments that I'm never going to need."

After the doctor had departed with the tearful and apologetic Robbie, Kirsty bundled the children into the pick-up. Back at Refuge, she sent them to feed the guinea pigs while she took time in the house to coax the fire into life, and collect her overall.

When she arrived at the stable, Minna was sitting happily on the straw nursing the cavies, while Timothy — with the nonchalant air of one who is thoroughly used to farm life — placed hay and hedge browsings in the racks for the goats.

"Shall I do the concentrate, Miss — a pound each, is it, and some of that old cabbage stuff?"

Kirsty hid a smile. Here he was at nine years old, airing his meagre knowledge to bolster his male ego in front of a young female — a fact which had clearly escaped the one that he was attempting to impress.

The work completed, Kirsty regarded her young charges.

"Decision time. Do we play inside for an hour, or do we go for a walk in the woods?"

"The woods, the woods." Both children set up an excited chorus.

"All right, calm down." She laughed. "I get the message. But if you want to see any animals — and this is a good time of day — you must be as quiet as mice."

The changes since Kirsty's last visit were remarkable.

It seemed little time since snow

had been on the ground and the scene undoubtedly wintery. Now the blackthorn hedge at the far side of the paddock was in bud and, in place of the snowdrops, clumps of sweet violet and primrose brightened the spaces between the trees.

They had covered a considerable distance before the children's silence was rewarded by the sight of an animal. Kirsty was delighted when, on top of a raised tree root, appeared a tiny shrew. For a moment it stood motionless, its long nose twitching, then away it scuttled to disappear among the undergrowth.

Minna, forgetful of their vow of silence, clapped her hands excitedly, causing a sudden flurry of activity. Out of the tree beside them, a jay rose on heavy laboured wings, its raucous cry filling the air, sending a rabbit, in the clearing ahead, bounding for cover.

"Time to go home," Kirsty told them a few minutes later. "We can come again another day."

Kirsty had no knowledge of Minna's normal daily routine, but decided on seven-thirty as a reasonable bedtime for a five-year-old.

She boiled the kettle and washed her with a bowl of warm water in front of the fire. Though bath and washbasin were fitted, the bathroom did not run to hot water and it seemed pointless to carry it upstairs.

"I'm afraid you'll have to share my bed for tonight, darling." Kirsty smiled, tucking her in with a rather battered blue teddy bear that she had picked up from Minna's own bed. "I hope there's room for me as well as you and teddy."

Minna smiled, hugging the bear. "His name is Winter."

Kirsty's brow wrinkled. "That's a funny name for a bear."

"Min Farbror says he's cold," the little girl explained seriously, "and that's why he's blue. He says I have to hug him tight to get him warm, and I do, but he never turns pink."

Kirsty laughed. "Never mind, love, he's very nice the way he is. Now I'll leave the light on, and come back to see you in a few minutes. All right?" She brushed a kiss on the soft hairline.

"'Night sweetheart."

Downstairs, she took up the bowl and towel and tipped the water down the sink.

"What's up with the old bird, then?"

Timothy lay sprawled in the armchair by the fire.

Facing the sink, Kirsty's face registered horror.

"If you mean what I think you mean, Timothy Hurst, you had better re-phrase it. Might I remind you that Mr. Amundsen's housekeeper was very kind to you. Anyway, I don't know. The doctors are going to test her to find out."

"This going to be permanent, then?" He nodded towards the stairs.

Kirsty looked up. "Permanent? Oh, I see — Minna. No, certainly not. Mr. Amundsen will be home tomorrow. Why?"

He sat up. "Funny kid, ain't she? You can say anyfing to her."

Kirsty turned, frowning. "What does that mean?" For once she was too concerned to make corrections.

He grinned. "She believes whatever you tell her."

Kirsty glared. "I hope, young man, that she believes you because you are speaking the truth. You're a lot older than Minna, and could teach her. I trust you haven't been filling her head with a lot of nonsense."

Timothy made no reply, and Kirsty decided to leave it at that for the moment. When she went back upstairs, a few minutes later, Minna was fast asleep, with the bear inside her nightdress.

2

THE little girl being in a strange, cold bed, Kirsty expected a tearful, disturbed night, but luck was on her side. Minna did not stir, either when Kirsty crept between the sheets, or when she slipped quietly away as dawn was breaking.

She completed her outside tasks before waking the children. For a moment only, Minna's face registered apprehension at her strange surroundings, then it was wreathed in smiles, as she held up her arms for a cuddle.

Patiently she stood while Kirsty brushed the tangles from her blonde curls and helped her to dress, and at the school gate — while Timothy raced away without a backward glance — she raised her face for a kiss, whispering in Kirsty's ear, "All the other girls have a Mummy — let's pretend you are my Mummy, shall we?"

It was a thought that remained with Kirsty as she busied herself later in Leif

Amundsen's kitchen, taking pork from the deep-freeze cabinet to de-frost in the microwave oven, while she sliced potatoes, and chopped carrots and leeks, to make the *Lapskaus*, a kind of country stew.

What had happened to the child's mother? In spite of his reference to his 'women', Leif seemed an honourable man. Certainly, she had heard no bad reports — even the brusque Jenny Carter seemed to have a soft spot for him. Had his future wife died before the wedding could take place — or changed her mind and left him, literally, holding the baby?

Kirsty set the lapskaus to cook in an earthenware crock in the wood-burning oven. There it would simmer while she turned her attention to the flatbrod. Finding none in the huge stone-floored pantry, she eventually unearthed the correct ingredients from a variety of bins, and set to work.

Busy with her thoughts, it did not seem long before she was wrapping the cooled cake in a napkin; placing it on the crisp blue linen tablecloth. What a pleasure to lay out the fine cutlery and glassware, and what an anti-climax when, propping a note against the cruet set, she left all the luxury behind, to return to her own primitive establishment.

She changed into her overalls reluctantly. Working all morning in such elegant surroundings, she felt even more ridiculous than usual in the well-worn masculine garb; coupled with which she was struggling to put away the thought that a life at Tall Trees as the wife of this fascinating Scandinavian, and as the mother of his sweet little daughter, would be a most enviable position.

At noon, way behind her usual schedule, Kirsty took herself sharply in hand. "Stop this nonsense! Get on with improving your own place, for goodness sake, and forget about him."

Having thus set her mind to the jobs in hand, Kirsty viewed the house with a critical eye. It was clear to see why the bedroom wall was damp.

About a yard from the windows the guttering had come loose, and there was a green mark on the wall where the rain had been running down behind. The bracket, apparently complete with metal fixing pin, was hanging free. Surely it would be a simple task to re-fix it?

About to step on the flat-runged ladder that she had found in the barn, Kirsty stopped. She might be able to climb like a cat, but not in these boots! Slipping them off, she made her way up the ladder in stockinged feet. A closer inspection of the place showed that the mortar between the blocks of stone, where the pin had been fixed, had worn into a slot, allowing the pin to drop out.

Kirsty made a mental note. A tiny bit of cement, some small pieces of stone, and a hammer. That would do it.

She was back up the ladder, absorbed in the task of putting the finishing touches to her handiwork, when the slam of a door heralded a horrified shout from the now familiar voice. "What do you think you are doing?"

She grinned down at him. "Enjoying myself."

He snorted. "Are you trying to kill yourself? Come down from there."

Kirsty put her hands together, and gave a mock oriental bow.

"To hear is to obey, O Master. I was

coming down, anyway."

Carefully making the descent, she was startled by another shout.

"Where are your shoes?"

Her eyes twinkling, she jabbed a finger downwards, then laughed aloud as his eyes rolled to heaven. Slotting her feet into the boots, she moved to stand beside him. "What do you think of that, then — good, eh?"

He glared down at her. "It would not have been good if you had fallen."

She narrowed her eyes. "Oh ye of little faith. I think it's a job well done — especially if my bedroom dries out as a result."

"Even so," he lectured, "it would have been more sensible to employ a builder to do it."

"Not if I couldn't pay him." She moved across to the house door. "Time for coffee?"

He consulted his watch, then nodded. "Yes, please."

Ducking his head to come through the doorway, he regarded her thoughtfully. "So you have to do all your own repairs?"

She smiled. "That's right. Unlike you,

103

Mr. Amundsen, I don't have an income."

He looked amused. "None at all?"

★ ★ ★

Kirsty put her hands on her hips. "You Scandinavians smile in all the wrong places."

He shrugged. "But you are not serious."

She raised her eyebrows. "I am, you know. The allowance that I get for Timothy doesn't always cover the damage he creates, so my bank balance is sinking fast into oblivion."

He frowned. "Then you cannot live, unless . . . "

"Something turns up?" She smiled at his serious expression. "But it will, never fear. Consider the lilies of the field Mr. Amundsen."

Suddenly, she laughed. "Tell you one thing — they certainly weren't arrayed like one of these!" And she spread her hands wide, showing off her working gear.

He shook his head at her. "You are . . . I do not know how to describe you!"

Kirsty grinned. "Incorrigible is a good word." She moved across to where he waited by the table. "Sit down — I intend to. These boots are killing me."

Leif leaned back to view her feet under the table. "They are too heavy for you."

Kirsty nodded. "And size eight — in other words, about three sizes too large — but never look a gift horse in the mouth, and beggars can't be choosers, and all such suitable proverbs. They will suffice for the time being. Now, how was the lapskaus?"

He grinned, and said something in Norwegian.

She blinked. "I learned the cooking, not the language. Was it good?"

He nodded his blond head vigorously. "Perfect. I enjoyed it very much."

Kirsty smiled. "Great. You never really know, do you, when you learn something, whether they are teaching you to do it exactly as it should be done?"

"You learn at your mother's knee, perhaps?"

She shook her head. "No, unfortunately. My mother died when I was born."

For a moment he dropped his intense gaze, turning the mug in his huge brown hands. "How sad."

Kirsty shrugged. "I didn't know her, so I was perfectly happy travelling with my father on all his expeditions."

His head jerked up and he leaned his powerful body forward, blue eyes sparkling in a face suddenly alive. "You visit Norway?"

She gave her head another little shake. "No, I've never been anywhere near your part of the world. My father's pet subjects were amphibians and insects, so to make his films we always went to warmer climes."

He leaned back, seeming disappointed. "Then I do not see . . . "

"How I came to learn the art of Norwegian cookery?" Kirsty gave a laugh. "Ah, well, it's all connected indirectly. You see, my Aunt Lydia — my mother's elder sister — didn't approve of my father. To others, he was a well-respected scientist — to her, he was a good-for-nothing beachcomber. So you can imagine her reaction, after Mother died, when he announced that he was going to take me around with him. Aunt Lydia nearly went beserk. Young 'gels' should be learning the finer accomplishments of life, she said, not grubbing around like wild animals in the jungle."

She hesitated, took a sip of coffee, and seeing that he still seemed interested, went on. "Father pretended to take no notice but, in fact, he took her words very much to heart — with the result that I did all the normal schooling while we were away, and when in England I was subjected to a wide variety of condensed courses: deportment and elocution, music and art, sewing and cookery. And I had to excel, because that way Aunt Lydia would be appeased."

His usually serious mouth curved upward. "And she was?"

"'Fraid not. When it came to the crunch, the pupil forgot she was supposed to be a refined young lady and called her a walking gasometer — she was rather an obese lady. So I was sent on my way, never to darken her door again!"

She looked up and, as their eyes met, she gave a rueful little laugh. "I suppose it was a punishment richly deserved, but

I did have some provocation. My world had just collapsed about my ears, and to throw insults about the man who had always been the centre of it was pretty bad timing, wouldn't you say?"

Leif nodded. "Yes. It's not easy to lose someone very dear to you."

Kirsty sighed. "Especially when it happens to be the only one you've got. My teaching went on, of course. I'd not learned everything by ten years old! Father's money was left entirely for my education, and I tried to take it all in, for his sake. So here I am — a veritable mine of useless accomplishments and scarcely a penny to my name."

"Ah," He glanced at his watch, pushed back his chair, and stood for a moment, looking down at her. "There I do not agree. An accomplishment may seem useless, but you cannot tell if, at any time, it may be needed." He smiled suddenly. "I have reason to be grateful for one of them."

She followed him to the door. "What about your evening meal — would you like me to . . . ?"

He held up his hand. "Not at all,

thank you. Did you not know that I'm a warlock in the kitchen?"

Kirsty blinked, then dissolved into laughter. "Wizard, you mean. I think a warlock is something different. I had no idea that you could cook."

A gleam of mischief came into his blue eyes. "I do not say cook. In the kitchen I make the smorbror."

"Open sandwiches. Anyone can do those," she said derisively.

He ducked out of the doorway, then straightened to his full height, the sun glinting on his blond head and beard, framing his shadowed face with light. "We are far more inventive than the English when it comes to smorbror."

Kirsty nodded. "So I've heard. You'll have to try them on me sometime."

It was a simple unthinking remark, quickly seized upon by Leif. An arm above the doorway, he leaned towards her. "You are thinking of a candlelit supper for two?"

Kirsty quickly side-stepped. "I'm thinking of a mid-day snack for one. This is Kirsty Trensham, not Leila Fennel, remember."

Leif rocked back, hooking his thumbs in the back of his belt, his piercing eyes scrutinising her from head to toe.

"No," he pronounced at length, "you are not at all like Leila."

For a moment longer, he considered her thoughtfully, then appeared to come to a decision. "Yes," he said, nodding.

Puzzled, she followed him to the gate, but he said nothing more until he was seated in the Range Rover. Then he leaned from the window.

"I must go into Malton. Is all right if the boy is late?"

"How late?"

He considered. "About an hour — perhaps a little more."

"Oh, that's all right. I thought perhaps you decided to dine out after all, so as not to put Minna at risk with your culinary arts."

Leif narrowed his eyes, but failed to hide the small gleam of amusement and, recognising it, Kirsty said, "One of these days, I shall make you laugh, Mr. Amundsen."

Deliberately he pulled his thick eyebrows together in a frown, and shook his head at her. Then he turned the key, raised his hand in salute, and sped off towards Rondale.

Kirsty hurried across the yard. If Timothy was going to be late, she might be able to fit in another maintenance job between feeding the stock and the evening meal. The yard was by far the worst feature of Refuge Farm. Kirsty surveyed it thoughtfully. Several tons of gravel on the surface would not have come amiss had finances allowed. The next best thing would be broken brick or chalk, and there was plenty of that around the place.

"It's hard labour, all right," she said to herself, getting stiffly to her feet for about the tenth time. Her back ached, her knees were sore, and the beginnings of blisters showed clearly on her right hand, but there was no doubt that she was getting there.

At first Kirsty planned to work on the scheme until Leif returned with Timothy but, in the end, the fading light and her own depleting energy were the deciding factors.

In the house, she made herself a cup of coffee, and leaned back wearily in the chair by the fire. A few minutes' rest, and she would take off the overalls and change into something a little more normal. Leif and Timothy would not expect her to be wearing the uniform of a labourer at this time of day.

"Are you there, Miss?"

Kirsty's eyes opened and she sat forward, blinking, for a moment completely disorientated. What was she doing, sleeping by the fire in her working clothes — and at this time. If it came to that, what was the time?

As if he could read her mind, Timothy answered the question.

"Mr. A. says he's sorry it's past eight o'clock, Miss, instead of five o'clock, as he said." He stopped, peering at her closely. "You been asleep?"

Kirsty nodded guiltily. "I'm afraid I have. I think I worked too long. I kept thinking that you would be coming home to stop me and, when you didn't, I carried on longer than I originally intended. What have you been doing all this time — you must be starving!"

Timothy grinned. "I was, Miss, but Mr. A. bought us all a Chinese — look,

112

he sent one for you, an' all."

"As well," corrected Kirsty, "but he shouldn't have done that. I've got enough food here."

"He said it would have all gone cold by now, and you could eat this as soon as I brought it. Come on, Miss, it's ace. It's got chicken and rice and chestnuts — and it cost more'n a pound each!"

Kirsty groaned. "Don't tell me. I shall be forever in that man's debt."

Timothy hopped from one foot to the other, watching her open the top of the foil dish. As the steam rose up, he jabbed a finger towards the food. "Look, that's a chestnut, and them's beans."

Kirsty laughed. "All right. I can see what they are. Would you like some more?"

The boy sighed. "Can't eat any more, Miss."

She smiled at his rueful expression. "Never mind. Tell you what, there's too much here for me. Suppose I eat half, and save the other half to warm up for you tomorrow?"

Timothy's eyes shone. "Oh, Miss, that'd be brilliant."

"Now," she said, sitting down at the table, "tell me what you've been doing this evening?"

"First we went for the boots," he told her importantly, "but we had to go to lots of different places, 'cos they didn't have none small enough."

"If they didn't have none, they must have had some," she teased.

Timothy looked confused. "They didn't — honest, Miss. Like I said, they was all too big."

"So you couldn't get any, then?" Kirsty decided to waive further grammatical explanation.

He nodded. "We did in the end, Miss. They're green, like Mr. A's."

Kirsty smiled, thinking of Minna. "Boots like her beloved Farbror. Minna would like that."

He laughed. "They wasn't for Minna, Miss. They was for you."

"Me?" Kirsty's own smile faded.

"Yes, Miss. They're in that parcel over there."

He indicated a parcel on the floor by

the door and, sure enough, when Kirsty opened it, there lay a pair of green wellingtons.

She stared from the boots to Timothy. "Did he say anything? I mean, I don't understand why he's done this."

Timothy shrugged. "Dunno. 'Spect he fancies you. Shall I ask him?"

"No!" Kirsty looked up quickly. "I'll speak to him myself. What else did you do while you were out?"

"Nuffin'. Just went to the hospital for Robbie."

Kirsty frowned. "Mr. Amundsen hasn't brought her home today, surely?"

Timothy nodded. "Yes, he has, Miss. He's got one of them phones what's got no wires, and they rang up while we was out and said to fetch her, but when he got there she wasn't ready. They was ages fitting this collar thing she's got to wear, and Mr. A. was real mad 'cos he had a date. He said she wouldn't wait, and she didn't, neither."

Kirsty snorted. "I hope he didn't blame it on poor Robbie. It's not her fault if he chooses girl friends who have no patience."

115

The boy grinned. "You got patience, Miss."

She frowned down at him. "Me? What have I got to do with it?"

As his grin widened, and she perceived his meaning, Kirsty glared.

"This conversation has gone far enough. Bed, young man, this minute, or you'll find that I have less patience than you think."

★ ★ ★

After his departure, Kirsty sat on for a few moments, in the chair by the fire. What an odd story Timothy told. Leif had a date? Feasible enough, but surely it wasn't customary in Norway for a young man to take along his housekeeper and two children? Besides, when Leif had set off, he had been wearing his usual working clothes.

And then there were the boots. Surely he had not taken her remarks that afternoon as a hidden request for financial assistance? No sooner had the thought crossed her mind than the telephone was in her hand.

The telephone rang for a considerable time before he answered, and his voice, when it came, was unusually agitated.

"Why have you bought me some boots?" Kirsty asked without any preliminaries or greeting.

His voice softened. "You are kind to Minna and Robbie."

"You are kind to me and Timothy," she told him. "I haven't bought you any boots."

"I do not need any. You do — you tell me so this afternoon." He seemed amused.

"I wasn't asking you to buy them for me. I can get what I need for myself."

"How? You have no income." He sounded smug, and Kirsty bristled.

"Not by taking charity, that's for sure."

"Ah, you are independent." He was laughing, she was sure of it.

"Yes, I am independent, Mr. Amundsen. I'm afraid I must ask you to take the boots back."

"And if I do not?" Suddenly his tone was serious.

"There's no question of that, Mr. Amundsen. There's no reason for you to buy them for me. I told you once before that I wasn't asking for your help."

"On the contrary, Miss Trensham . . . " Now the voice was calm and cold . . . "there is every reason. Since you do not accept the boots as a gift from a friend, you can consider them a reward for labour. I, too, am independent, you see. You have done me a service, and I will pay."

There was a loud click in her ear, and the dialling tone returned.

"Damn!" Kirsty slammed down her own receiver. How stupid she'd been. She'd been very glad of his help in the past. Her pride had caused a rift, and what had she to be proud of? Not only had she alienated her most considerate neighbour, she hadn't asked about Robbie, or thanked him for the take-away meal. She couldn't insist on returning that — she'd already eaten half of it!

Ring him again. That was the answer. Say all the things she ought to have said the first time.

With trepidation, she dialled the number and, once again, several moments passed before it was answered. "Leif Amundsen."

"Oh, it's me again, Kirsty, I . . . "

"There's nothing further to say." His words were out, and the receiver replaced.

Slowly she put the telephone back on the rest. That was it, then. No apology or explanation possible — nothing she could do to breach the gap of her own making.

3

WHILST Leif continued to transport Timothy to and from school, Kirsty scarcely caught a glimpse of him during the next few days. Several times she hurried forward as he stopped the Range Rover, but the moment he saw her approaching he would accelerate away, leaving her more deflated than ever.

On Friday morning, the day of the supposed transportation of Gigi and her offspring to Jenny Carter at Westfield, Kirsty expected a short visit, or curt telephone call, to inform her of the arrangements. She received none.

When at last the telephone did ring, at around two o'clock, she was so relieved that she dived upon it at once.

"Oh, Jenny, thank goodness. I was beginning to think you'd all forgotten. What are the arrangements?"

There was a marked silence at the other end.

"Are you there, Jenny?"

"It's Tim's mother."

Kirsty blinked. "Yes, Mrs. Hurst?"

"I'm taking him home for a bit. Want him to meet his new father, see? There's a train at four."

Kirsty hesitated. "This is arranged with the Social Services, I take it?"

"What's it got to do with the welfare?" The voice began to sound antagonistic. "I'm his mother, ain't I?"

"Yes, of course, but since you've left him in care, they must check where he is at all times. I'll have to advise them of your request, Mrs. Hurst, so if you will give me your number, I'll do that at once, and ring you back in a few minutes."

"It's a call-box."

Kirsty frowned. "In that case, would you give me ten minutes, and then call me back, Mrs. Hurst?"

The caller agreed and, the moment she rang off, Kirsty put in a call to Sarah who, in turn, rang her superior. To her dismay, the outcome was a sanction for the request. Timothy's mother had unlimited access, and had taken the boy home on a number of occasions.

121

"Let's hope she keeps him this time," was the comment from higher circles.

Kirsty did not agree. Mischevious though he was, she had become fond of Timothy and, for some inexplicable reason, she had a bad feeling about this visit.

Forced to comply with Mrs. Hurst's request to put him on the four o'clock train, she had to act fast. The train was from Malton, not Rondale. If Timothy left school at three-thirty, as usual, it would hardly leave enough time for the journey.

Her hasty telephone call to the school was followed quickly by another. If Leif was good enough to provide transport, in spite of the rift in their relationship, the least she could do was to inform him of the change of circumstances.

It was nevertheless a relief when Robbie answered.

"I really have a lot to be thankful for," the older woman admitted, in reply to Kirsty's enquiry about her health. "They tell me that as long as I wear this collar I'll be fine, and I know that it could have been something much worse than

122

an arthritic joint causing the trouble but, oh, my dear, it does make things so difficult with my head in this position all the time."

"I can appreciate that," Kirsty sympathised, "I only wish that I dare come to help you. No doubt Mr. Amundsen has told you about the trouble between us?"

"He has, my dear," Robbie sounded thoughtful. "Tell me, would you have reacted the same way if he had given you flowers?"

"Well, of course not." Kirsty was indignant. "That would be different, wouldn't it?"

"Would it, my dear?"

For a moment there was silence, then Kirsty sighed. "No, you're right. I thought he was handing out charity, due to the remarks that I had made previously. Instead it was a simple gesture of appreciation in a practical form, wasn't it? That's what he meant when he said that I was not at all like Leila." The laughter came suddenly back into her voice. "Of course, you realise that this means I have to apologise — and he's going to be so arrogant about it."

Robbie laughed. "I have a feeling you can handle him very well."

Kirsty was not so sure. Hurrying away to pack Timothy's case, she was completely at a loss to know how she would make the approach — if, indeed, she was ever to be given the chance.

"I'm coming back, aren't I, Miss?" Timothy leaned from the train window, his expression wistful.

Kirsty gave a reassuring smile. "Of course you are. Half your clothes are here — and Turnip, don't forget. I can't do with you being away for too long."

The train shuddered and began slowly to move.

"Have a good time!" She waved and tried to look cheerful

All the way home, Kirsty could not get the pathetic little face out of her mind. He had been so eager to go on previous occasions, expecting to stay permanently with his mother — wanting to. If only she could rid herself of the premonition that something was amiss.

Parking the pick-up in the yard, her thoughts still full of the boy, she was startled as the quiet evening air was shattered by a raucous voice from the stable. Snatching open the door, she was confronted by the prettiest little goat blinking innocently over the top of the rails one minute and howling like a banshee the next.

The note from Jenny was, as before, short and to the point: Milk Gertie before Mabel. Be firm! J.C.

Sound advice indeed. Whereas Gertie had always been the quietest of creatures, Mabel seemed the most awkward. Determined not to be milked by this stranger, she kicked, sat down or jumped forward, turning the whole procedure into a battle of wills. Each time, Kirsty made her stand again, but by the time the job was done, she was fit for nothing but dragging herself back to the house and soon to bed, dreading the thought of going through the whole process again the next morning.

Her fears were unfounded. The next day Mabel was like a different animal, quietly obedient.

Relieved that all went well, Kirsty was nevertheless deflated when the morning routine was done. It was Saturday.

Normally Timothy would have been behind her at every step, under her feet as she cleared away the milking utensils, sitting on the step with Turnip as she came through the door with the bucket. Without his constant prattle, the place seemed desolate, and Kirsty felt unable to settle down and tackle any of the jobs on her maintenance list.

Abandoning any thought of self-discipline, she changed the working clothes for her blue coat, and set off to find Westfield. A visit to Jenny Carter might give her the incentive to carry on with the good work.

Westfield lay at the far side of Fennel Farm Associates. Within half-an-hour Kirsty was stepping out of the pick-up on to a clean swept yard.

There were two banks of goat houses. Jenny, hard at work in the further one, indicated a man feeding a kid. "My brother Harry. You'll have met him before."

Kirsty nodded. He was the man who rode his bicycle to Tall Trees, and who had gone with Leif to recover the pick-up.

"Well, don't just stand there, young woman. There's a clean overall on the door."

Smiling good-naturedly, Kirsty removed her coat. Soon she was in the thick of it, feeding the kids with a bottle, milking goats of assorted shapes and sizes, filling hay racks and water buckets.

The goats' milk at Westfield was not simply cooled for use as it was at her own place. In the low stone building nearest to the house, several cheese-cloths hung over buckets, separating curds and whey for making yoghurt cheese. More milk was carried into the house to simmer on the Aga, for the first stage of making the yoghurt itself.

"You've certainly got a flourishing little business here. Makes my efforts at Refuge look a bit paltry," remarked Kirsty, slipping on her coat for the reluctant journey home.

Jenny snorted. "Not for long, if that Fennel woman gets her way, I'll be bound."

Kirsty frowned. "Leila Fennel? What has she to do with it?"

The older woman turned off the tap,

and reached for the towel. "It's her land — or will be in a month when the lease runs out. Fevershams always said there'd be the option to renew, and Harry says it'll be no different, but she's been sniffing round with that baboon Pratley a sight too much for my liking. She's hankering to turn us off, you mark my words, young woman."

Kirsty regarded her thoughtfully. "What will you do, if she does?"

Reaching for her crutches, Jenny shrugged. "Been here on this place all our lives, Harry and me. Don't know what we'd do, and that's a fact."

Driving down the road towards the village, Kirsty's thoughts were full of Jenny. She was feeling to some extent responsible for the situation. It had been clear on her arrival that Leila Fennel had included Refuge Farm in her plans. Thwarted, had she decided to take Westfield from Harry and Jenny Carter instead?

It was past noon when she arrived back at Refuge. Clicking the gate shut, she surveyed the patched yard and green-streaked walls gloomily. She studied the sky. Up at Westfield, some of the goats were out. Gertie and Mabel would surely benefit from a spell in the paddock.

Twenty minutes later, while the goats explored their new confine, Kirsty was back in overalls, crouching on the floor of one of the outbuildings, sorting through tins of paint. She was thankful that Albert Turner had been such a prudent man. He appeared to have kept everything from white distemper to black bitumen. The unfortunate thing was that there was not one colour in anything like a usable quantity.

Lifting out a tin of white wall-coating, she measured the depth with her eye, and surveyed the walls. Not enough, as it was, to cover even one side of the house, but surely she had seen the decorators at the children's home thinning this stuff with water? She grinned. Oh well, give it a whirl. If it ran off the walls, at least it would cover the patchy ground!

Soon she was up the ladder, armed with a brush, slapping on the gritty substance as fast as she could go.

It was easier than she expected, and the result, she decided, as she put the finishing strokes to the front wall on the main section of the house, some two hours later, was fantastic. With the marks covered, the wall looked good and solid, not old, and in need of repair, as it had done before.

True, the indented pantry wall, not to mention the stable and other single-story buildings, looked grey in comparison, but there was no doubt that this was the face-lift that the old house needed.

The remainder would have to wait until tomorrow. The air was becoming cool, and it was time to put the goats back into the stable.

Now, she must try to obtain news of Timothy.

"Kirsty!" Sarah sounded surprised to hear from her. "I was going to ring you. What news of Timothy?"

"Good question," said Kirsty. "I was about to ask you the same one."

"He hasn't been in touch?" Sarah's voice took on a rather anxious note.

Kirsty's brow wrinkled. "He only went yesterday, Sarah. I hardly expected it. Can you tell me how long he's supposed to be away?"

"There was no definite arrangement," her friend told her. "It all depends on how he gets along with the new stepfather."

"Stepfather? His mother has actually married this one?"

Sarah sighed. "I'm afraid so, but I don't like him. I don't quite know why. If you met him, Kirsty, you'd know what I mean. He has plenty of money so, naturally, the mother dotes on him and, since she still has parental control, there's little we can do. All we can hope is that, if things do go wrong, the boy himself will get in touch with us."

Kirsty went to bed early, but slept badly and rose with a dull headache, feeling even less like work than on the previous morning. Sipping her first coffee of the day, she peered from the window. It was a light, blustery morning, too early yet to feed the stock. A walk in the woods might blow away the cobwebs.

★ ★ ★

Her first stop was to admire the blackthorn hedge. In bud when she

131

had walked with Minna and Timothy, it was now a picture, the profusion of white blossoms covering every vestige of spiked branch. In the woods, too, the sights and sounds of spring were everywhere.

Here and there among the trees gorse bushes, previously unnoticed, stood brilliantly yellow, and the new leaves on the sycamore were beginning to unfurl.

Stooping to examine a tiny clump of wood anemone, Kirsty was startled by the sounds of movement ahead. She crept forward, peering through a mass of golden willow catkins into a small glade — prepared to see almost anything but what was actually there.

On the grass knelt the unmistakable form of Leif Amundsen. His left hand restraining a small furry body, he plucked at something with his right, speaking softly all the time in his native tongue. Whatever was he doing — and whatever was he doing here? Afraid to disturb him, Kirsty remained motionless.

Suddenly Leif's hand jerked up, and at the same moment, he released the hold with his left. With a sharp wriggle, the animal regained its feet and, as it bounded away among the trees, Kirsty saw that it was a baby rabbit.

Leif sat back on his heels, laughing aloud. Then he began to coil up a length of wire, dragging it from the undergrowth and, to her amazement, completed the operation by throwing the coil over the barbed wire fence on to Leila Fennel's land.

Slowly he began to move forward, away from where Kirsty was positioned, his feet dragging in the grass, eyes cast downward. He had covered a few yards thus, when he dropped suddenly to a crouching position, thrusting his hand into a patch of deep fern. When he removed it, he was grasping another length of wire, which he dealt with in the same way.

A sudden shaking of the branches made her switch her gaze to where she had last seen Leif. She stared, amazed, to see him hanging by both hands from a thick branch and, as she watched, he swung a foot out on to the top of a fence stake, letting go of the branch to make a neat landing over the other side of the barbed wire. Frowning, he gazed about him at the fallen trees of the once-beautiful copse, before marching stiffly away.

For the remainder of her walk, Kirsty puzzled over what she had seen. Leif was a considerable distance away from home. Were these visits to her woods a regular occurence — or had he spent the night with Leila Fennel, and merely wandered out in this direction for an early morning constitutional?

On the return journey, Kirsty took her secateurs from her pocket to clip a few twigs of willow from the densest portion of the bush. It would benefit from the thinning, and the bright catkins would grace her table with a cheerful glow.

Reaching the yard, she was surprised to find Jenny Carter waiting.

"Thought you were still a-bed, young woman," Jenny greeted her. "Harry dropped me off. Brought you this." She held out a cloth-wrapped bundle.

Kirsty opened it delightedly. "Yoghurt cheese. Oh, how delicious. You are good to me." Impulsively, she brushed a kiss on the older woman's cheek.

"You're too soft, young woman,"

Jenny turned quickly away, but not before Kirsty had seen the little smile playing about her lips. She looked round. "Where's that young man this morning?"

"Timothy?" Kirsty opened the door, and they went inside. "Didn't I tell you yesterday? He's visiting his mother — at least I think it's just a visit. If he stays and I don't get the board allowance cheque any more, I'll be looking for a job."

"Young Leif's advertising."

The unexpected statement took Kirsty by surprise. "Advertising?"

"For help in the house. Good job for you, young woman."

Kirsty sighed. "Might have been if I hadn't been so adamant about neighbours helping each other without thought of payment."

Jenny roared with laughter. "Put your foot in it good and proper, have you? He'll still give you a job, if you ask him."

"Beg for it, you mean." Kirsty was indignant. "I can just imagine how arrogant he'd be."

135

"Then you don't know him," came the terse reply.

Kirsty was not about to put her theory to the test. Diplomatically, she changed the subject.

"I'm getting along all right with Mabel — after winning the initial battle!"

Jenny nodded approval. "That's the ticket. Show her you intend to be boss and she'll accept it. She's a bit like Houdini, mind. Leave a loophole and she'll find it. You'll need to watch her when she's out."

As she finished speaking, a car horn sounded outside, and Jenny got awkwardly to her feet. "Time to get cracking. Tell me when you've finished the cheese and I'll send some more. Oh . . . " she turned back . . . "keep it in a china bowl, under a plate. It doesn't take too kindly to airtight plastic boxes."

"Thank you very much. I'll remember." Kirsty waved to Harry, and watched until the Range Rover was out of sight.

Now she was late, and both goats and guinea pigs were reminding her that the day was clear and fine, and she had much to do. With no more delays, her plan went well — at first. By lunchtime, she had painted the remaining house walls and, stopping only for a glass of milk, she turned her attention to the woodwork.

To her surprise and satisfaction, the result of mixing all the gloss paint together was a rather attractive chocolate brown. Her efforts in utilising it were not so pleasing — she found the paint thick and difficult to apply.

★ ★ ★

Exactly a week later, returning wearily to the house after yet another spell of painting, she was still wondering when Timothy's return was going to be. At the risk of sounding like a mother-hen she decided to make further enquiries, and phoned the home.

"Funny time to ring, I know," she apologised, the moment that Sarah lifted the receiver, "but I'm having a short rest. I'm exhausted. What news of Timothy?"

"The worst, I'm afraid." Sarah was suddenly serious. "He's missing. For reasons of his own, Timothy let down the tyres on his stepfather's car, then took off. I've had the man here demanding that I give Timothy up, and I was very pleased I hadn't got him."

"You've informed the police, of course?"

"Of course," Sarah sighed. "They're looking for Timothy, but it seems they have nothing on the stepfather, and since my thoughts on the subject are only assumptions . . . " She hesitated a moment. "Look, Kirsty, I know it sounds stupid, but you be careful. It's obvious that the boy will run to you — and that man knows where you are."

Kirsty made a valiant effort at nonchalance. "Well, it would seem the man has good reason to be angry. Anyway, I'll be all right, Sarah. You know me."

"Yes, I do know you." Sarah could not be fooled so easily. "Too independent by half. If you'll take my advice, you'll tell your nearest neighbour."

Kirsty didn't relish going to Leif to tell him that she might be in need of protection from a man she had never met. He would think it was some silly prank.

In spite of the disquieting news, Kirsty slept better that Sunday night than she had for over a week. Waking refreshed, she was even more certain that there was nothing to fear. This conviction did not prevent a sudden surge of apprehension when, in the middle of the morning, a car stopped at the gate, and a stranger approached.

"Craven," he introduced himself. "Ministry of Agriculture. Thought it about time I let you know I'm here if you need any advice about your woodland."

Although Mr. Craven took time and trouble to sort out Kirsty's queries on the care of the trees, it seemed to her from the outset that his main concern was the havoc wrought by Leila Fennel on the other side of the fence. Could that be why he had come — to check on the work being done and report it?

Deep in thought, Kirsty was halfway back across the paddock on their return journey before what she had seen registered in her mind. Gertie in the corner, happily cudding. Gertie only — so where was

Mabel? A check of the hedges revealed a small gap on the roadside boundary.

Bidding a hasty farewell to Mr. Craven, she jumped in the pick-up and set off anxiously in the direction of Tall Trees. Goats were apt to get themselves in the most terrible trouble when roaming loose, and she had little doubt that Mabel would uphold the tradition admirably.

As she arrived at the bridge, without sight or sound of the truant, there came an unexpected roll of thunder. Kirsty turned the vehicle round. If she started in the other direction, she might catch up with Mabel before the rain came, and the irate neighbours reached the shotgun stage!

Her hopes faded when she saw the group by Leila Fennel's gate. Wasn't it just typical that everyone was there to witness her disgrace? Easily recognisable, even from a distance, were Mr. Pratley and Leif Amundsen and, as she drew nearer, she could make out Leila Fennel standing between them.

All three were surveying the remaining shreds of two formerly flourishing broom shrubs which, contained in brass-bound barrels, had graced either side of the entrance. The mournful noise from the confines of Leif's Range Rover confirmed her suspicion that shame and humiliation were about to be piled upon her head.

Pulling up her hood against the sudden squally wind, she cast a glance at the darkening sky. Gertie was still in the paddock — at least, it was to be hoped so. Best get the apologies over as quickly as possible, and be on her way.

"It's all right for some, Mabel," she grumbled, glancing in the back of the Range Rover. "You get the tasty morsels, and I get the humble pie!"

She stopped, peering more closely at the goat. The light was fading, but surely . . . ? As the animal moved forward, giving her a clearer view, Kirsty stared, spluttered, and then began to laugh uncontrollably, leaning against the vehicle for support.

Her mirth was brought to a sudden halt by the outraged Leila Fennel, whose voice was little less than a shriek as she stormed towards her.

"Laugh, would you, you stupid girl? Wait till you get the bill, and see if you think that's funny. I took you for a fool the first time I saw you, and I was right. People like you are nothing but a damned nuisance, and the sooner you pack your bags and clear off, the better it will be for all of us. I tell you . . . "

The ranting voice went on and on. Kirsty stood silently, aware of the others approaching, watching the scarlet mouth open and close, yet no longer listening to the actual words. What a spiteful woman this Leila Fennel was. How could such a person as Leif Amundsen become involved with her?

A drop of rain on Kirsty's hand snapped her out of her trance. This was not her concern, and it was time she said so. "Miss Fennel . . . " she began.

There was not a break, not the slightest pause, in the stream of insults being thrown. She tried again.

"Please listen, Miss Fennel."

It was no use. Calmly, Kirsty turned towards Leif. "When your girl friend sees fit to take a breath, you might inform her that she's wasting it. I've neither the time or the patience to wait for the end of this monologue." She turned away.

"Where do you think you're going?" A hand snatched at her shoulder, scarlet-tipped nails digging into the flesh.

Kirsty prised up the fingers, lifting the hand away as if it were some undesirable object.

"Home, Miss Fennel," she informed her, without turning round.

"Not yet, you don't." Leila leapt forward to block her path. "I want an apology, and some arrangement about settlement — in front of witnesses."

Kirsty's wide hazel eyes met the narrowed ones of her assailant steadily. "Apology, Miss Fennel? Settlement? I don't really think I owe you either."

Leila glared. "And why not, pray?"

Kirsty glanced past the group at the stumps of broom, and back again. "I suppose you did actually see this particular goat eating the broom?"

Leila's face turned puce. "Yes we did. It was that goat, and that goat alone, so don't you try to wriggle out of it, you little . . . "

Kirsty held up a finger. "Temper, temper. I should save a few of those

143

insults if I were you — you're going to need them in a little while. As for me, it's not my concern whether the animal ate your shrubs. The goat in the back of Mr. Amundsen's vehicle is not mine!"

The scarlet mouth dropped open. "Not yours?"

Kirsty smiled. "That's right, Miss Fennel. I have a goat missing — a pretty little brown and white one. The one you have here is much larger, and all-white. Nothing to do with me at all. Sorry." She turned away. "'Bye for now, everyone. I'll see you all sometime, I expect."

★ ★ ★

Once on her way, Kirsty's first concern was to get back to Refuge and put Gertie under cover. Fortunately, after the first few drops, the rain held off and soon she was leading the quiet creature into the warmth and safety of the stable. The moment she stepped inside, she collapsed into laughter.

There, happily eating the hay straight from the bale, stood Mabel. Blinking

144

innocently, as if nothing untoward had occurred, she came forward to nuzzle Gertie for a moment, then moved calmly towards her pen.

Kirsty shook her head. "You animals will be the death of me yet."

Giving a quick look round to make sure that all was in order, she closed the door and hastened towards the clothes line. The sky was fast filling in again. If the rain came as threatened, the laundry would be back to the dripping stage in a matter of moments.

At the middle of the line, Kirsty could only just reach the pegs. Turning round, with the intention of slackening the rope, she collided with Leif before she was aware of his presence. Startled, she jumped and her face drained of colour. Then, recognising his tall stature, she gave a sigh of relief.

"Oh, it's you. Thank goodness. I didn't hear anyone come in."

He lifted the next two pegs from the line, and tossed the garment on top of the others. "I am sorry if I startled you. I have come to apologise for Leila."

"Why?" Clear hazel eyes looked steadily up into his own. "Has she lost her voice, or are you her keeper?"

His jaw tightened. "Neither."

"Anyway . . . " she smiled . . . "I wanted to see you. I've an apology of my own to make."

"An apology?"

"You bought me a gift the other day. I should have thanked you, but instead I was rude. I'm afraid my stubborn independence is always getting me into trouble. I really am sorry."

"It's not necessary for you to apologise. It was clearly a misunderstanding." He smiled suddenly. "Do the boots fit?"

"Perfectly, thank you." Returning the smile, she held out a foot for his inspection. "And it's not necessary for you to apologise, either. Miss Fennel should do her own apologising."

He lifted another peg from the line. "Leila has not a calm disposition. Is not an easy time for either of us."

"Or me."

One hand still on the line, his quizzical blue eyes stared down.

"I've a couple of worries of my own. I

don't go round shouting abuse," she said calmly.

He looked away, reaching for the last peg. "You are different. Leila is easily upset."

"So I have to take it, do I?" Kirsty's eyes flashed.

He gave no answer and, raising her head, Kirsty found that he was standing with his arms outstretched, holding up her nightdress to look up and down its length. White lace, and threaded with blue ribbon, it was Kirsty's one item of pure extravagance.

She struggled to conceal her amusement. "Do you like it?"

He looked down, then back at his raised arms. Suddenly he seemed to realise what he was doing and, to her astonishment, he blushed.

Carefully dropping the garment into the basket, he turned so quickly that she hardly caught the murmured words. "It's very pretty."

Deliberately, to ease his embarrassment, she laughed. "No need to be amazed, Mr. Amundsen. I do have some pretty clothes to wear, when I'm not feeding and milking goats."

He moved towards the gate and, picking up the basket, Kirsty followed.

"Your goat has returned?" he asked politely.

She laughed again. "In the stable, happily chewing the hay when I got back."

He nodded. "I have returned the other to Jenny."

Kirsty stared. "Jenny?"

Leif gave a little shrug. "Of course. Since it is not your own, you must know that it belongs to Jenny."

Kirsty's expression registered dismay. "I should have done, but I didn't think. Leila's right — I am stupid. I ought to have said it was mine; she would never have known. After all, what can she do to me?"

Leif looked faintly amused. "You seek to protect Jenny Carter?"

The emphasis was on the first word. Kirsty bristled.

"A clown like you, you mean, don't you — so why not say it? Leila did."

He turned sharply. "I do not say it, because I . . . " He broke off as a screech of brakes heralded Leila Fennel's sports car.

Kirsty grinned. "Talk of the devil . . . "

Leif gave her a warning scowl, and she turned to watch Leila come forward, two high spots of colour on her cheeks indicating her mood.

"There you are, Leif. I've been trying to ring you. I felt sure you would be home by now."

Leif opened the gate. "I did not expect you to need me in so short a time. I stopped for a moment to speak to Miss Trensham."

"More than a moment, it would seem," Leila scoffed. "We have to go immediately. Shall we use your car?"

He nodded. "Ja. It's faster." Suddenly, he seemed weary.

"I'll follow you up, then."

Kirsty smiled. "Good idea. Make sure he doesn't get lost again."

No one answered, and Leif was moving off towards his vehicle when Leila suddenly turned to Kirsty, still standing with her clothes basket on her hip.

"And I'll thank you to keep that child off my land."

Kirsty frowned. "Child?"

"That ragamuffin you've seen fit to give a home to."

Kirsty's eyes flashed. "If you mean Timothy, he's not here."

Leila glared. "I know he's not here. I've just seen him skulking round my place."

About to ease himself into the Range Rover, Leif turned. "I do not think it could be the same child, Leila. What Miss Trensham means is that Timothy is away visiting his mother. Is that not correct, Miss Trensham?"

Kirsty nodded. "I put him on the train myself."

"Well, if you say so," Leila spoke grudgingly. "Come along, Leif."

"Good day, Miss Trensham," Leif called.

Kirsty turned back. "Good day, Mr. Amundsen. Good day, Miss Fennel. Have a nice time."

★ ★ ★

Back in the house, Kirsty dumped the laundry on the table and went straight to the telephone. Fennel Farm Associates lay between her own place and Westfield. If Leila Fennel had seen Timothy he could be at Jenny Carter's place at this very moment.

Her decision to keep the matter to herself had to be reversed. The wisest course of action now was to take Jenny into her confidence, and persuade her to keep the boy, if he showed up, while the situation was clarified and the danger — if any — was past.

Apprehensive as to the outcome of the conversation — Jenny was unused to children — Kirsty was surprised to find her a staunch ally.

"Good thing to have a boy about the place while I'm in plaster," she assured Kirsty, "and don't worry about the stepfather. I'll soon pepper his rump if he comes sniffing."

Three days passed with no advancement on any front. Going about her daily business, Kirsty was aware of Leila Fennel travelling one way past her gate, and Leif passing in the other, but neither called.

Kirsty was surprised to find that she

missed Leif's visits. She had become used to his comments — even his criticism — and with no one to show an interest either way, there was little pleasure to be derived from the maintenance work. Sheer determination made her keep going, sanding down and painting woodwork, filling the gap in the hedge, clearing undergrowth and pruning trees in the wood.

Yet when the telephone call that she was expecting finally came, it was still a surprise.

"Timothy's here — you'd best come over." Jenny's message was brief and to the point. "And bring a change of clothes."

Kirsty put the goats back into the stable, threw some clothes into a bag, and departed. Timothy had been missing for five days, and it took little imagination to realise in what condition both boy and clothes would be in.

"In the shed, milking the goat, if you please." Jenny's words as Kirsty came through the door, made her look at Timothy in dismay.

"Oh, Tim, you really shouldn't . . . "

"He was hungry." Jenny leapt in his defence. "What would you do if you hadn't had a square meal for days?"

Clearly, she was not angry, and Kirsty smiled with relief. "The very same, I should think. Now let's get you cleaned up, young man. On your feet."

As he eased himself out of the chair, Jenny threw Kirsty a warning glance. The boy could hardly stand, and it was not simply the lack of nourishment which was the cause of the trouble; he was a mass of bruises.

"Who did this, Tim?" Carefully, Kirsty eased his shirt back on to his shoulders.

"Me Step-Dad, Miss." Far from his usual perky self, the boy was near to tears.

"But why, love? What had you done?"

Timothy sniffed. "We went to this jeweller's shop. Me dad kept the man talking and I was supposed to pinch stuff out of the shop, only I was too scared, Miss. There was this other man watching me, so I ran back home and told me mum. When me dad came home, he was real mad and he hit me. Mum said I'd better go back with him next day, and no cheek, so when they'd gone to bed, I ran away."

The moment the boy had been gently cleaned-up and was more comfortable, Kirsty rang the doctor and the police.

★ ★ ★

When she explained the situation, they and the social services approved the plan to leave the boy at Westfield for the time being. He was not fit to attend school, and it was decided that his presence in the community should be disclosed to no one. Sergeant Ryan suggested, in addition, that he ring Kirsty at pre-arranged times to check on her welfare. It was his theory that Timothy's stepfather would already be making his way to Refuge Farm, seeking the boy to prevent him telling his story, and in the event of his not being apprehended beforehand, could well be in an ugly mood when he arrived.

Kirsty could not have been more in agreement. Although she left Westfield giving the appearance of lightheartedness, she was in fact more than a little alarmed

154

at the possibility of facing such a brutal man in the seclusion of her own home. Had it not been so vital to maintain the utmost secrecy regarding Timothy's whereabouts, she would have been tempted to ask if she, too, could stay with the Carters.

As it was, it could well be that Timothy's safety depended upon her going about her daily business as if the boy were not present in the area and, to that end, she must remain at Refuge.

It was decided that Kirsty should not visit Westfield at all. Harry would act as go-between as he passed on his way to work. The plan had a double advantage for Kirsty. Not only did it provide another check on her welfare, it was also an opportunity for her to keep abreast of local events, particularly the comings and goings at Tall Trees.

"Making ourselves scarce today." Harry grinned, hopping off his bicycle one morning, four days after Timothy's return. "Too many womenfolk about."

"Womenfolk?" Kirsty stepped up on to the gate. "Why, what's going on?"

Harry groaned. "Interviews, lass. About

half a dozen of 'em, wanting to look after the bairn, and such."

Kirsty laughed. "You are an old grouch. They want to help."

"Help themselves, more like." Easing himself back into the saddle, Harry snorted. "Got their eyes on the gaffer, I reckon, most of 'em."

Strange as it seemed, the thought rankled. It was almost as if she viewed the job applicants as competitors for his favours, which was ridiculous. There was not the slightest chance that she would ever be anything but a source of amusement to Leif Amundsen, with or without a new housekeeper.

Halfway through the day, unable to think of anything else, she took herself across the room to stand, glaring in the mirror. "If you are so concerned about who goes to work in Leif Amundsen's house, why didn't you go after the job yourself? It's too late now, so just forget it," she told herself.

It was easier said than done. Five o'clock saw her hovering in the yard, waiting for Harry to pass by on his way home.

156

"Well . . . " she hopped up on to the gate, as soon as he appeared . . . "who got it?"

"What's that, lass?" Clearly Harry had forgotten their morning conversation.

"The job," she reminded him, "in the house."

He shrugged. "Don't know, lass. Been up at the top end all day, marking out a section of the broad leaf for pollarding. Leif thought we'd give it a try up there, on account of all the animals. Fond of the wild-life he is, being a zoo man."

"Zoo man? Leif?"

He nodded. "Set his heart on working with animals, had young Leif. Took it at University, and came out top of his year. Pity in a way — still, he's made a grand job of Tall Trees, and that's a fact."

He glanced along the road. "Well, best not be keeping Jenny waiting with tea. See you tomorrow." And off he pedalled.

Kirsty stepped down, and slowly crossed to the stable. What a surprising man this Leif Amundsen was. A degree in zoology was a little awe-inspiring.

The week passed with no further news,

and it was an odd and lonely weekend. The telephone conversations with Jenny, Timothy, Sarah, and Sergeant Ryan, did not make up for the fact that, from Friday evening to Monday morning, she was entirely alone.

Even the company of her beloved animals did little to cheer her and when, on the Sunday evening, a magnificent veteran Bentley passed her gate with Leif at the wheel, and Leila beside him, Kirsty was pitched into the blackest despair. For the first time for many years, she crept to bed in tears.

* * *

On Monday morning, opening her eyes to a beautiful spring day, Kirsty felt thoroughly ashamed of herself. She leapt from her bed. She would not allow that man to dominate her thoughts a moment longer.

An hour later, coming back from the paddock after turning the goats out, Kirsty was just in time to see a lorry pull away from the farm gate. She hurried across the yard, and was amazed to find a load of gravel dumped outside.

"Oh, no!" Snatching at the delivery note, stuffed in the gate, Kirsty groaned. "It should be at Westfield."

It seemed a long time before Jenny answered the telephone.

"Ah, there you are." Kirsty sighed with profound relief. "Sorry if you were outside. Someone has delivered a load of gravel here — I think it's yours."

"Didn't you see Harry?" Jenny sounded impatient.

"Yes." Kirsty's thoughts went back to their conversation. "He was telling me that Miss Robertson still hasn't chosen an assistant housekeeper."

"Men!" exclaimed Jenny in disgust. "Talk about anything but what's important. He was supposed to tell you the gravel was coming."

Kirsty grinned. "To you or to me?"

"To you. I suppose he said nothing about the letter, either?" Now she sounded exasperated.

"Letter?" Kirsty frowned. "No, I'm afraid not. Look, Jenny, what is all this about?"

"No time to explain now." Jenny was

clearly in a hurry. "Put it on your yard, and see Harry about it." And down went the receiver.

The gravel was incredibly heavy. If there had been any possibility of starting at the far side and clearing the portion which was actually on the road, she would have attempted to move only half of it that day. As it was, the gateway was completely blocked and, until she had moved almost threequarters of the pile, so was the road.

As usual, Kirsty made the best of a bad job, laughing at her own weakness. So what if a barrow-load was too heavy to push? She would carry half barrow-loads, even quarters. The job would be done eventually.

Eventually was a good word. She had been right to use it. She leaned weakly against the gatepost to survey her efforts. Eleven o'clock, and she had just forged a way through at the side of the gate.

It was a tedious job, but how wonderful it would look when it was finished. No more squelching black mud to wallow through. She'd be able to milk the goats in her high heels!

Keeping her mind busy to encourage her tired body to carry on working, Kirsty nearly jumped out of her skin when a car horn sounded right behind her.

"What on earth do you think you are doing — blocking the road, like this?"

As the voice heralded the arrival of Leila Fennel, in her sports car, Kirsty decided that — of the two sounds — the horn was the more musical.

"I've another shovel in the shed, if you feel like lending a hand?" She grinned, patting her waistline. "Good for the figure, you know."

'A mistake. Definitely a mistake, Kirsty' she thought. 'Your neighbour has turned puce. Hit on a raw subject, no doubt.'

"Not that you need it, Miss Fennel." 'Hasty placatory remark. Too hasty. The facial hue has deepened. Now she thinks you are being sarcastic.'

"I'm sorry about this," Kirsty decided that an apology was in order. "I'm clearing it as quickly as I can."

"Not quickly enough!" Leila reversed the car sharply with a squeal of tyres, and sped off in the direction from which she had come.

"Wait for it!" Kirsty gazed after her. Two minutes to get home, a one-minute telephone call, plus another two minutes for the journey from Tall Trees. Five minutes at the most and she would have Leila's Viking lord down on her like a ton of bricks.

Oh, well. She shrugged. There was nothing she could do to improve matters in that space of time.

She had transported only one load when the expected happened but, instead of her Norwegian neighbour, it was Harry Carter who climbed from the driving seat. Suddenly she realised how much the bright spring day had darkened and, as he approached, the first big drops of rain began to fall.

Harry took the shovel from her hands, glancing up at the sky. "I'll move it, lass, and you spread it."

Kirsty took up the rake. "What is all this about, Harry? Why am I wearing myself out shovelling gravel that I didn't order, and that you've paid for?"

He looked up. "Miss Fennel's putting

us out, lass. Not renewing the lease. Westfield is going on the market at fifty-five thousand."

The short explanation was all that Kirsty was to get until they had finished the job in hand. Harry wheeled, Kirsty raked, and the rain became steadily worse, but within half-an-hour the task was completed.

"Coming in for a drink, Harry?" Kirsty was feeling fit to drop.

Harry, twice her age, looked as fresh as a daisy. He shook his head. "Best get back. Three loads of timber to go today, and with Leif not there . . . "

"Not there?" Kirsty looked up in surprise. "I thought Leila was rushing to see him."

Harry grinned. "No doubt she was. Most likely, he crept off last night without telling her."

Last night? So he had been away since then. Leila Fennel was not the only pebble on the beach, it would seem.

She walked with Harry to the Range Rover. "Fifty-five thousand pounds is a bit steep, isn't it?"

Harry sighed. "Too steep for us, lass.

Can't do it. Forgot all about the gravel until last night. Jenny and me, we didn't see the point of putting it down on her place."

★ ★ ★

When he had gone, Kirsty sat at the table leaning on her elbows, her chin in her cupped hands. Physically tired, she was also unusually depressed.

Never look a gift horse in the mouth, they said. She doubted the truth of that statement. Money isn't everything, they said. Slightly more believable — but what a lot it could have done for her, right now. Two people who, in the short space of time that she had known them, had shown her nothing but kindness, were being persecuted. What would she have done without them to take the goats, and look after Timothy? Now they desperately needed help, and there was nothing she could do.

The first idea came to her in the late afternoon when she was leading the goats back to the stable. She telephoned Jenny who read her the official letter.

164

"So what about my place? The yard is already yours, anyway." Kirsty suggested.

"Your place?" Jenny was blank. "I don't follow you, lass."

"I know it's not as big as Westfield . . ." Kirsty warmed to her plan . . . "but your sheds would probably go on the paddock, and . . . "

"And where would you be all this time?"

Where indeed? The Carters had proved firm friends, but Kirsty had little faith that she and Jenny would be compatible in one kitchen.

"Back in the city." She made a brave attempt at enthusiasm.

"And hating every minute of it." Jenny was her usual down-to-earth self. "I'm not blind, young woman."

Kirsty sighed. "Well, what other solution is there? I suppose I daren't suggest a mortgage?"

"Not if you value our good relations. Harry and me have never borrowed money in our lives, and we don't intend to start now."

She was on dangerous ground. "How do you feel about rented property, then?"

Kirsty said cautiously.

Jenny sighed. "Jump at it, lass, if there was any — that could be paid for in advance, same as the lease — but we can't have what isn't there."

Kirsty pondered the words long after the telephone receiver was replaced. Was there no way, nothing she could devise to help her friends?

4

IN the morning, out of the blue, came
the answer. More correctly, it was an
idea which, if agreed upon, could
provide the answer.

Before she had time to consider it
further — before she had time to dodge
the issue — she got out of bed, went to
the telephone, and dialled the number.
It was just six-thirty.

"Leif Amundsen." The receiver was
lifted at once.

She swallowed nervously. "Good
morning, Mr. Amundsen. It's Kirsty
Trensham."

"Miss Trensham?" The usual, slightly
mocking tone. "This is indeed an
honour."

"For whom, Mr. Amundsen, you or
me?"

"For me, naturally," the dry, half-
amused voice came back. "A call from
you so early in the morning. A call from
you at all . . . "

"Reserve your judgement."

"Ah." There was a moment's pause. "There is a hidden snag."

"There is indeed." So far, so good.

"I am listening, Miss Trensham."

Kirsty took a deep breath. This was it.

"I understand that the position of assistant housekeeper at Tall Trees is not yet filled — is this correct?"

"That is so." he sounded surprised. "But this is more Robbie's department than my own. If you are interested, I can ask her to . . . "

"No, Mr. Amundsen," Kirsty was quick to qualify. "Thank you, but it would serve no purpose for me to see Robbie in the first instance. I have a slightly different proposition in mind — one to which she certainly could not agree on your behalf."

"I see." He was clearly intrigued. "Then I had better grant you an interview myself, Miss Trensham. I shall be in my office all the afternoon."

"I'd rather ask you now."

She could almost see the raised eyebrows. "Business before breakfast?

There is a reason, of course?"

"Of course."

"And it is?"

"Simply that I am ringing you because I dare not face you and say what I have the courage to say over the telephone."

There was a small silence. Then, "An honest answer. You are afraid of me?"

She gave a little laugh. "Not in the normal way, but you know I don't like asking favours, and this is a big one."

"Then you had better state your proposition, Miss Trensham."

Kirsty's hand shook, and she gripped the receiver harder. It was now or never. Best get on with it, and take the consequences.

"Thank you, Mr. Amundsen. The proposition is this: I will come and work in the house for you, for an indefinite period, and for no salary, if you will do something in return."

He gave a low whistle. "An indefinite period, and no salary? What, may I ask, is this great favour that you would like me to do in return?"

"Buy a farm."

The silence was deafening.

"Buy a farm?" At last he found his voice. "But I have Tall Trees. I do not need another place."

"I know. If you did, there would be no need for me to attempt bribery."

"It is your farm, Miss Trensham?"

"Oh, no." The question took her by surprise. "It's bigger than my place."

"Ah, so you wish to expand?"

"Expand? No . . . " Kirsty was horrified . . . "I'm not asking you to buy it for me. It would be entirely your own property, the rent due to you — nothing to do with me at all."

He let out a long breath. "It is early, Miss Trensham, and I seem to have missed the main point of this conversation."

"Namely, what do I get out of the deal?"

"Ja, just so."

"The farm is occupied by two people who have been — and are being — very good to me. I would have the satisfaction of seeing them able to remain unharrassed in the place where they have lived all their lives."

"That is all?" His tone showed incredulity.

"Isn't it enough? They are being forced out of their home, Mr. Amundsen, the only one they have ever known." Trying to impress on him the urgency of the situation, Kirsty was fighting rising emotion. "If I could buy the place myself, I would — but I can't. I just don't have the money. I offered them my place, but I knew they wouldn't accept. Do you think if I could have come up with any other feasible solution that I would be talking to you now?"

"All right, Miss Trensham."

The calm words, coming without pause after her impassioned outburst, took her by surprise, and she failed to interpret their meaning.

"All right? What do you mean — all right?"

"I mean, Miss Trensham, that first thing this morning I will instruct my solicitor to look into the matter and, should it prove a viable investment, I will give it my urgent consideration."

Kirsty gasped. "You mean you'll do it? You'll actually do it?"

"In so far as I've already said."

"But you'll try — that's the point — you'll try." The tears which had been welling into her eyes brimmed over, and ran down her cheeks. Kirsty sniffed. "Thank you, Mr. Amundsen. You won't regret it, I promise. Even if nothing comes of it, I'll still keep to my end of the bargain."

"If I did not know you better, Miss Trensham, I might easily believe that you are crying."

Kirsty sniffed again. "Perhaps you don't know me as well as you think."

"Perhaps it's something that I should remedy." He hesitated a moment, and then spoke briskly. "But, to business. This establishment has an address, I take it?"

"Oh, yes, I'm sorry. It's Westfield."

"Rondale?" There was a low thud, as if he had been leaning back in his chair and moved his weight suddenly forward. "But that is Harry Carter's place."

"That's right." Kirsty swallowed. "Does it make any difference?"

"Only that there must be some mistake, Miss Trensham. Westfield has for many

172

years been under lease."

She found herself nodding. "Which term expires shortly, and is not to be renewed. The farm is for sale, Mr. Amundsen. Jenny Carter read Miss Fennel's official letter to me over the telephone."

"So they tell their troubles to you but not to me." He sounded disappointed.

"For an obvious reason, I would think."

"What's that?"

"They told me," she explained, "as a friend who is as powerless as they are themselves. You, Mr. Amundsen, are in a position to do something about it. To tell you would be tantamount to asking for help."

He sighed. "And they are independent people."

"They certainly are . . . " Kirsty managed a little laugh . . . "which is why I'm ringing you at this time, so that no one else will know."

"So it is to be our little secret?"

"If you wouldn't mind. Then there's no danger of them finding out, and feeling obligated. Would ten o'clock be all right, do you think?"

"Ten o'clock, Miss Trensham?"

"For me to start this morning — if Robbie thinks I would be suitable. I could be earlier in future but, to be honest, I wasn't geared up for you to accept."

To her surprise he laughed. "It would seem that you do not know me, either, Miss Trensham. I shall speak to Robbie, and ask her to ring you. From that moment on, I shall expect my household to be the epitome of efficiency."

"It shall be done, Mr. Amundsen. I promise that you'll not even be aware of me. Thank you for giving me so much of your time."

He gave a small laugh. "I shall have reason to thank you for a longer period, I think. Good day, Miss Trensham. Robbie will call you later." Kirsty replaced the receiver, leapt to her feet and delightedly threw her arms up into the air. She glanced at the clock. Seven-fifteen. Time to get down to work. In two and a half hours, she would need to be ready to start her first journey to Tall Trees as an employee. Robbie's call came at nine.

Worried that her arrangement with Leif himself might be misconstrued by the older woman, Kirsty was pleased to find her enthusiastic about the suggestion. No need for an earlier start, she said, ten o'clock would be fine, and if she could manage to stay until half past three . . . ?

Kirsty couldn't believe that everything was falling into place so easily. The hours seemed short, leaving ample time to tend her stock and fulfil her own household requirements. Nevertheless, she arrived at Tall Trees that first morning in a state of considerable trepidation. Leif, there was no doubt, would fulfil his side of the bargain to her complete satisfaction. Could she do the same in return? The promise to work for an indefinite period, without salary, was worthwhile only if she could prove herself indispensible. Whether or not that ambition would be achieved, it was plain that the addition of another pair of hands at Tall Trees was very necessary indeed. The surgical collar, holding her head erect, made even the most simple task difficult for Robbie.

★ ★ ★

Kirsty took over completely — without asking and without argument. Thoroughly experienced in running an establishment with twelve children, she swept through the smaller household with ease, packing lunch baskets for the workers, making beds, dusting, polishing, cleaning floors — finding, as she did so, an unexpected bonus for her labours.

The large windows, overlooking the courtyard, garden, and one stretch of the river, allowed her to observe Leif Amundsen on his home ground for the first time — a fact which served only to increase her admiration for him. Whatever he tackled Leif Amundsen was completely in charge of every situation; not only popular with his employees, but clearly respected by them.

Beautiful surroundings, and an abundance of pleasant company, were his for the taking. What conceit to think that Kirsty Trensham could have anything to offer which would add to his comfort. A close observance of his everyday life brought her own insignificance sharply home. She must keep strictly to her place, observe her vow to remain unseen, and make no contact with her employer.

Kirsty's last requirement of the day was the preparation of light tea for Minna, and a more substantial evening meal for all three occupants of the household. The menu being Robbie's decision, it was simply a matter of following her orders.

"I could collect Minna from school every day, and supervise her tea, to save Mr. Amundsen breaking off."

It was three-fifteen, and Leif had just reversed the Range Rover out of the barn.

Robbie made to shake her head, then screwed her eyes tight, smiling. "I must remember not to attempt these sudden movements. I was about to say, my dear, that much as he would appreciate your thoughtfulness, Mr. Leif likes to spend as much time with Minna as he can manage." She laughed suddenly. "Afternoon tea is usually a time for high jinks. I'm often left wondering which is the child, I can tell you." Kirsty left for home at three-thirty, still bemused by this insight into Leif's character. Kind and gentle though he had always been with the child, there had never been the slightest suggestion of horse-play. It was nice to think that he did on occasion let his hair down, if only in the confines of his own home.

★ ★ ★

By the end of the week, Kirsty was arriving at Tall Trees in a happy, relaxed frame of mind. Her duties were clear, and so easily managed in the time allowed that on some days she was looking for something extra to occupy her last half-hour.

Such a day was the Friday of her second week there. At three o'clock, Minna's tea laid, the casserole prepared, and Robbie dozing by the fire, Kirsty peeped round the door of the one room in the house that she had never entered — the office.

Her intention to give it one sweep of the eye, and then retire to a safe distance, was broken the moment she opened the door.

On the mantelpiece was a photograph. Younger, beardless, there was still no question about the fact that it was Leif: Leif as she suddenly remembered him from all those years ago, standing at the gate of Refuge Farm, the water from the hosepipe in her hand dripping from the ends of his hair.

Was it possible that he had recognised her straight away as the errant child? If so, there was little wonder that he had considered her something of a fool from the very beginning of their acquaintance. Restoring the beautiful frame to its former position, her eye was taken by a matching frame, at the other side of the clock. The girl was beautiful. Her blonde hair, in a plait over one shoulder, the sparkling eyes and wide smile, brought the photograph so much to life that Kirsty could hardly take her eyes away. There was little doubt that this was Minna's mother. She had thought that the child resembled Leif, but the smile on this girl's face was so like Minna's, it was uncanny.

What was she doing? Suddenly Kirsty realised that she was inside the room, prying into intensely personal possessions.

Turning swiftly towards the door, her skirt swirled, catching in something on a chair. The next moment a pale blue file slid to the floor, scattering papers in all directions. She knelt on the carpet, frantically gathering them together in awkward, trembling hands. Thank goodness they were not personal papers. Letters, orders, receipts, all referred to the timber trade.

She was sorting them into what she hoped was the right order, when the telephone on the desk shrilled into life. Tentatively, she lifted the receiver.

"Tall Trees. Kirsty Trensham speaking."

"Ah." The masculine voice was brisk. "Walker Brothers here. You have our order of the fifth?"

The blue file! She had seen the letter heading. Come on, Kirsty. Assume an air of efficiency. "If you'll wait a moment, I'll check. The fifth. Ah, there it was. "Yes, I have it here."

"We'd like to double it, and take delivery a week early."

"I think I'd better get Mr. Amundsen in on this one. I'll try to contact him."

Frantically, she tried to call Leif on the

180

portable telephone. There was no reply.

"I'm sorry. I can't seem to raise Mr. Amundsen. I'll make sure that he gets your message, and . . . "

"I'm afraid I need to know this afternoon, so I can work out some prices. Pity." The voice seemed resigned. "I would have liked to do business with you. What a shame."

"Could you give me an hour?" Kirsty spoke quickly. This seemed like a big order, and Leif was about to lose it.

"An hour?" There was a pause. "Yes, I think I can manage that." Kirsty took down the details in her small, neat hand. She was about to wake Robbie when one of the big timber lorries reversed past the window. No doubt Leif would be there to supervise the loading. She was wrong. It was Harry Carter who came forward, pursing his lips as she explained. "Should be able to do it, lass, but we can't go ahead without young Leif's O.K."

Kirsty sighed. "And you have no idea where he is, I suppose?"

Watching the lorry closely as it reversed slowly towards the opening, Harry grinned.

181

"Called to Miss Fennel's, just after eight-thirty this morning. Ring him there, lass — if you dare!"

Did she dare? As she reached for the receiver, the bell rang underneath her hand, and before she had lifted it to her ear, the voice came. Masculine again — and foreign.

"Hello. Dette er . . . "

"I'm very sorry. I'm the only one here at the moment."

The caller hesitated, then spoke again, clearly puzzled. "Er det . . . ?"

"Tall Trees, yes." Kirsty rushed to explain, "but I don't live here."

"This is Herr Amundsen. I . . . have need to . . . to . . . "

She must help him out. "Herr Amundsen, I see. I'm afraid that your son isn't here, but I was just about to ring him and would be happy to give him a message."

"Ja. Thank you, Miss . . . ?"

"Oh, sorry, didn't I say?" Kirsty apologised hastily. "It's Trensham. Kirsty Trensham. I am Leif's . . . Mr. Amundsen's . . . nearest neighbour."

"Ah, Miss Trensham. You have the goats, ja?"

She sighed. "Oh, dear. Has he told you about me? Just when I was trying to pass myself off as a sensible human being. Still, I really am capable of passing on a message, Herr Amundsen."

He laughed. "Say to Leif . . . please . . . I telephone."

"Today?" She must get the message right.

"Ja . . . today . . . later."

She smiled. "Yes, I can do that for you, Herr Amundsen. It has been nice talking to you. Thank you for ringing. God dag."

Deliberately, she gave her farewell in his own language. He seemed pleased.

"God dag, Miss Trensham. I speak to you again, perhaps?"

★ ★ ★

She replaced the receiver, but a glance at the clock made her lift it again at once.

"I'm sorry to trouble you, Miss Fennel." Kirsty spoke in her most respectful tone, as Leila answered her call. "Kirsty Trensham here. Does Mr. Amundsen happen to be with you?"

183

"He does." No offer to call him to the telephone.

"May I have a word with him, please?"

"Really! This is most inconvenient."

"I'm sorry, but it is rather urgent."

The telephone banged down, and for a short time there was silence.

Then it rattled again. "Leif Amundsen."

"Ah, Mr. Amundsen, I won't keep you a moment. We've had a call from Walker Brothers regarding their order of the fifth, received by us on the seventh . . . "

"Who is this, please?" Leif was puzzled.

"It's Kirsty Trensham, speaking from Tall Trees."

"Miss Trensham? But you sound so different."

"It's my super-efficient secretary image." Kirsty laughed. "Don't worry about it. Now, this order, Mr. Amundsen. I'll just run down it to refresh your memory."

Taking up a pencil, she checked off each item as she read down the page. "That's the original order," she finished, "but Mr. Walker would like to double it, and take delivery a week early. He needs an answer this afternoon."

"I think that should be in order, Miss Trensham." Leif sounded pleased. "You have arranged for me to telephone him?"

"No need for you to bother, Mr. Amundsen. I'll see to it." Kirsty peered at the clock. "And I must do so immediately. I've already taken up some time talking to your father."

"My father, Miss Trensham?"

"Yes. He asked me to tell you that he would be ringing again. Now, presumably, we confirm the Walker Brothers order by letter?"

"Yes, but . . . ?" Evidently he was still finding it difficult to believe in this new organised neighbour.

Kirsty stifled a laugh, and kept her voice cool and efficient. "I'll leave it on your desk, ready for signature. Oh, one other thing, Mr. Amundsen. Have you remembered to collect Minna from school?"

"Yes, she is here now, Miss Trensham."

Kirsty smiled. "Goodbye then, Mr. Amundsen. I'm sorry to have disturbed you."

Replacing the receiver, she collapsed

185

into laughter. That would give him something to think about.

It took only a few minutes to make the telephone call, and type the short letter confirming the new order. Placing it on the blotter, she hurried to the kitchen to take her leave of Robbie.

"Mr. Leif has asked you about coming in tomorrow?"

By the door, Kirsty hesitated. "Saturday? No, but I can, easily. The usual time?"

"Make it any time you can spare, my dear." Robbie smiled. "We're all very grateful for everything you do."

★ ★ ★

Busy with her own housework that evening, it seemed to Kirsty that the telephone never stopped ringing.

First there was Sarah, wanting to know the latest news of Timothy. Then Jenny, informing her that Miss Fennel had a local buyer. Sergeant Ryan rang, checking on her welfare. And twice, Leif Amundsen, although the actual reason for his calls was obscure.

He asked her about coming to Tall

Trees the next day, yet seemed to know that it was already arranged. He praised her efficiency with the Walker Brothers order, and her neat setting out of the letter. He apologised for 'having to be out', remarking that she had been at Tall Trees for two weeks and he had not yet caught sight of her there. Both calls were almost identical, so that, after the second one, — around eleven o'clock — she was given the distinct impression that what he really wanted to say was the one thing left unsaid.

The next morning, Kirsty was up earlier than usual. She had little doubt that Gertie and Mabel took a dim view of being left to their own devices for so many hours in the day, and had decided that she must spend as much time with them as possible.

The goats had never been allowed in the woods. It was longer than she intended since she had been there. Under the trees, most of which were now in full leaf, it was quite green and shady. In the more open spaces, the ground was carpeted with a mass of wild plants and flowers. A horse chestnut, near to

CTL7

187

Leila Fennel's side of her land, was a profusion of white blossom and, from the branches of a nearby sycamore, a group of fledgeling blackbirds were testing out their wings.

Enchanted, Kirsty watched their tentative efforts, forgetful of her two companions until a munching sound made her turn quickly — to see Mabel devouring some low-placed, almost indistinguishable, beech flowers, to which she seemed particularly partial.

As they crossed the paddock on their return journey, the bright day darkened. No point in leaving either goats or laundry outside any longer. Soon she must be on her way.

Kirsty set off at once for Tall Trees, wondering throughout the journey where her elusive employer would be at the time of her arrival. Smiling, she contemplated his reaction at the first sight of her as she really was. In almost three month's acquaintance, he had yet to see her uncovered by boiler suit and woolly hat, oilskin and sou'wester, or simply hooded duffle coat — in each case her long hair pushed completely out of sight, the soft curves of her figure shrouded by ill-fitting garments.

Even to herself, she would not have admitted that her early start might have some connection with her thoughts. Had she done so, the shock of disappointment on finding that he had already left the house, might have been less keenly felt.

When Kirsty entered the kitchen, Minna was dancing about in her nightdress, while Robbie laid the table.

"I got up 'specially early to see min farbror off, but he had already gone." Padding across the floor in her slippers, Minna pouted.

"Especially early?" laughed Kirsty. "I have been up over three hours, young lady. Now, let's see if you can get dressed before breakfast is ready."

Minna's eyes sparkled. "Is it a race?"

"Yes," Kirsty told her. "Off you go, quick as a flash. No half measures, now. Cardigan and shoes fastened before you come down." The little girl set off, and Robbie smiled.

"She's been so excited, my dear, since I told her you were coming. Saturdays are rather boring for her when Mr. Leif is away." She sighed. "What will happen if . . . "

Kirsty waited. If what? Had Leif gone to Leila Fennel's again, so early in the morning? Clearly, he found it difficult to keep away, which gave rise to Robbie's half finished sentence. "What will happen if they marry?"

Robbie changed the subject, no doubt feeling that to question her employer's action was treading on dangerous ground.

★ ★ ★

From the moment that she had finished breakfast, Kirsty kept Minna occupied. Making beds, running over the floor with the vacuum cleaner, polishing windows — all were turned into a game, with a score point for whichever one finished their particular job first.

"I've won. I've won," sang Minna, tripping into the kitchen at eleven-thirty. "We've finished, and I beat Kirsty nearly every time." Robbie laughed. "Then I suspect that you were given the easiest tasks to do, young lady. Still, I think you both deserve a break, and as it happens, the kettle is just on the boil."

"Will Mr. Amundsen be in to lunch?" Kirsty tried to sound nonchalant. With a sigh, Robbie shook her head. "I doubt it, my dear. Mr. Carter tells me that there's no timber going out today — in fact, nothing of any urgency required for the remainder of the weekend. I would imagine that he'll take the chance to . . . " She hesitated, noting Minna's quickening interest. "To stay where he is," she finished. "He rang me last night," Kirsty told her. "Twice."

To her surprise, Robbie's face lit up. "He did, my dear?" Kirsty nodded. "The funny thing is, I don't really know why. It was almost as if he just wanted a chat."

The older woman waved her hand in a gesture of understanding. "No doubt he did. There's no better way to dispel depression than to have a few words with the right person."

The right person? Kirsty blinked. What on earth was Robbie talking about?

She was given little time to ponder. Already, Minna was pulling on her arm. "Tell Robbie about your monkey."

191

Kirsty laughed. "I had it as a pet when I was a little girl, on an expedition with my father. Minna tells me that Mr. Amundsen is going to buy her a horse."

Robbie nodded. "I shouldn't wonder, my dear. In some ways, he spoils her dreadfully. Still, it's understandable, in the circumstances."

★ ★ ★

There was little left to do once the dishes were cleared away and an evening meal prepared. Minna settled down to watch television, leaving Kirsty free to depart whenever she wished, but for once she felt in no particular hurry.

Accepting another coffee, she stayed chatting to Robbie, hoping for a meeting with the master of the house.

At four-thirty, she was forced reluctantly to take her leave. Her offer of working the next day had received profuse thanks but a firm refusal. It would now be into next week before she had any further contact with Leif. It was too much to hope that he would ring again.

Rounding the bend on the downward slope, Kirsty slowed to approach the bridge. There was something coming from the opposite direction; she would have to reverse.

The gleaming Volvo fast approaching could only be making for Tall Trees and, once on the bridge, there would be no room to pass. Kirsty pulled off the road, round the corner of the first stone pillar, waiting for the car to pass. It didn't come.

Slipping from the driving seat, she moved forward on foot and, once on the bridge, could see that the Volvo had stopped some distance ahead. A few steps further and the driver came into view, standing in the road, looking lost.

As Kirsty appeared, he hailed her.

"Excuse me." He held up a small sheet of paper in his hand.

Kirsty quickened her pace. "Can I help you?"

"I hope so." He indicated the paper. "I seem to have left my reading glasses in the office, and I can't make out the name of the place where I want to be."

Kirsty smiled, holding out her hand. "May I see?"

Taking the paper, she was surprised to see, written in a scrawling unfamiliar hand, Refuge Farm, Rondale."

"It's Refuge Farm." She gave him a puzzled glance. "My place."

"Then you must be Miss Trensham?"

"That's right." She handed back the paper. "What can I do for you?"

"I've come to collect Timothy Hurst."

"Collect him?" Eyes flicking over the stranger, noting the well-cut suit and rather too bright tie, Kirsty felt suddenly apprehensive. There was something odd about this man, something she couldn't quite put her finger on.

"That's right," he broke into her thoughts. "You'll have had a call from the welfare?"

The welfare. The name that Timothy's mother used for the social services. This man was no official. He was the bully of a stepfather.

"I'm afraid they've sent you on a wild goose chase," Kirsty hedged, feigning genuine regret. "Timothy isn't with me at the moment. He's visiting his mother for a while, and I really don't know when to expect him back. I don't even have his address, but if you ring Miss Marshall, at the children's home, she could give it to you."

He nodded. "Good idea. Perhaps I could ring from your house?"

Into Kirsty's mind flashed a picture of her kitchen, with Timothy's easily recognisable clothes draped all round the room to dry.

"I'm sorry. I'm not on the telephone at the farm." A quick answer, but a wrong one. Immediately, the man's expression changed.

"Strange that, Miss Trensham. I could have sworn you were — especially since my wife rang you there to ask for the boy." He took a step closer. "Time we stopped bluffing, don't you think? You know who I am, and what I can do if you don't tell me what I want to know. You've got the boy somewhere. Where is he?"

Blind panic made her lunge at him; a move which almost worked. The unexpected attack catching him off guard, he stumbled, but as she turned

195

to run back to the pick-up he shot out a hand, grabbing her long hair and twining it round his hand to yank her head backwards. "Tell me where he is!"

"No!" She stamped hard on the man's foot, but his grip on her hair tightened, and his free hand sliced across her face like a whiplash.

Kirsty let out a piercing scream, and it was at that precise moment of despair, when she thought all was lost, that someone else took events in hand.

"What in thunder is happening here?"

For a second, Kirsty was unable to comprehend that the rasping, furious tone didn't belong to Timothy's stepfather. It was only when an arm came round her assailant's neck, pulling him backwards and forcing him to loosen his hold on her, that she realised help was at hand. Yet her ordeal was not quite over.

Struggling furiously, fists doubled in an attempt to escape his captor, Timothy's stepfather flung out an arm in a wide arc towards Kirsty.

As the crashing blow contacted her ribs, she crumpled, gasping for breath, unable even to whimper, the tears flowing unchecked down her cheeks as she knelt on the ground clutching her arms round her bruised body. The stream of curses in a foreign tongue, the resounding smack of fist hitting flesh, the slam of a car door, all washed over her.

Suddenly all was silent. Kirsty didn't hear the approach, didn't know anyone was there until gentle hands came under her elbows.

"You can stand?"

Wordlessly, head bowed, she got to her feet.

"I . . . I've lost my shoe." Even to herself, her voice, when it did come between sobs, sounded strange.

"First I'll get you into the car, then I'll find your shoe." The voice was infinitely gentle.

Kirsty nodded, making no protest as he lifted her carefully on to a soft, deeply-padded seat.

"I'm afraid the heel is broken." Returning from his search, Leif placed the shoe into her limp hands.

"Does . . . doesn't matter." Kirsty was struggling to control the sobs, which would keep coming, making the pain worse. "Where is he?"

"In his car — out cold at the moment. I've used his tie to secure his hands to the steering wheel, and I have the car keys and the rotor arm in my possession. As soon as I've taken you home, I'll call the police."

"Th . . . thank you." Kirsty sniffed, and felt vainly in both pockets. No handkerchief, and what a sight she must look — eyes all puffy, and the corner of her mouth swollen and bleeding.

She became aware that he was proffering his own handkerchief. Gratefully, she accepted it, dabbing at her eyes, breathing in the tangy scent of his aftershave as she blew her nose.

"Thank you." Her voice still sounded strange and unnatural.

"That's better." He waited a moment in silence whilst she recovered a little of her composure. Then he said quietly, "It's not safe for you to travel unless you have the seat belt round you. May I?"

He leaned round her. "I won't fasten it too tightly. We haven't far to go, perhaps?"

"Where are you t . . . taking me?"

Kirsty was almost panting, afraid to take a deep breath.

He gave a soft little laugh. "To your home, if you would just tell me where that is? You need to see a doctor, have proper rest and care."

"Where it is? You know where it is." What was he talking about?

His voice came again, the tone both kind and apologetic. "It must be that I should recognise you. You live in the village, perhaps?"

He didn't know her. Did she look such a mess — totally unrecognisable? Of course not. In different circumstances she would have laughed. Wasn't this the first time he had seen her in woman's clothes, with her long hair loose — even showing at all? Her appearance must be totally different to the one that she usually presented to him.

Kirsty gasped out, "It's me, you ninny. Kirsty. Don't you know me?"

★ ★ ★

In the short silence that followed, Kirsty raised brimming hazel eyes to his astonished face. His lips were slightly parted, eyes open wide, as he stared back at her, completely mesmerised.

"Kirsty?" When finally he spoke her name, it was a whispered question, as if he was still unable to believe that the girl beside him could really be the one that he should know so well.

Then, suddenly, he snapped into action — switching on the engine, reversing the car round. "You are coming back to my home."

"No, Leif, I can't." She put a small hand quickly on his arm. "The goats . . . I'm late already."

His eyes raked her face, but he made no argument. Instead he turned the car again, keeping at a smooth steady pace until they drew to a halt at the gate of Refuge Farm.

When Kirsty made to open the door, he put out a restraining hand. "Just sit a moment," he said.

Uncurling himself from the driving seat, he opened the gate, pulling it wide in order to give enough room to drive in.

"The gravel has made a vast improvement," he remarked, as he alighted from the car a second time.

Kirsty nodded. The day she had laid it with Harry Carter she would have been ready to swear that she felt as stiff and sore as she ever could. Now she felt ten times worse.

Leif moved round the car to open the passenger door, holding out his hand. "You have your house key, Kirsty?"

Her lip quivered, and the tears welled into her eyes again, as she shook her head. "It's in my bag — in the pick-up, at the other side of the bridge."

He put a quick, comforting hand on her shoulder. "No matter. Everything needed to feed the stock, and to milk, is outside, yes?"

Blinking away the tears, she nodded. It was possible to see to the animals without going into the house.

"You are coming to watch — to make sure I do nothing wrong?" Leif was smiling down at her.

Kirsty's eyes widened. "You?"

"Of course, me." He gave his head a little shake of reproof. "You surely don't think I'd allow you to do it in your present condition?"

She dropped her gaze to her hands, still holding the broken shoe.

"To be honest, I don't feel that I could, just at the moment."

"Come on." His strong hand came under her elbow.

He led her into the stable, pulling forward a bale of hay. "Sit and rest for a moment. The goats are in the paddock?"

"Yes," Kirsty made to get up. "But I could be . . ."

"Sit down," he commanded. "You are going to do nothing at all."

Sitting silent and motionless, she watched him take the halters, too weary to think of anything but the present, until he returned with the goats.

He was an expert. If she had witnessed this scene beforehand, the degree in zoology would not have surprised her. Each task was dealt with quickly and efficiently, as if it was his everyday duty.

Moving her hand, Kirsty found herself touching Leif's jacket, thrown on the bale beside her. He was in his best clothes. Guiltily, she watched him fill, and re-fix, the water buckets — unable to summon energy enough to help, yet feeling that she should not allow him to do the work.

She crumpled his handkerchief in her hand. "I'm very sorry about all this, Mr. Amundsen."

He straightened up, leaning one arm on the rails, regarding her steadily over the top. "It's easy to tell that you feel a little better."

She frowned. "Why do you say that?"

He grinned. "You call me 'Mr. Amundsen.'"

"I always call you 'Mr. Amundsen'." Kirsty was puzzled.

He smiled, coming through the rail, closing the gate carefully.

"Not all the time. Just now, up the road, you call me two other things."

Kirsty's face paled. "What other things?" Her tone was apprehensive.

Leif put a hand to his cheek, raising his eyes upward in an attitude of deep thinking. "You say 'Leif' and . . . er . . . Ninny," he pronounced.

Surprised by his obvious amusement, she asked, "Didn't you mind?"

He sobered at once. "Leif — provided it allows me to continue to call you 'Kirsty' — I like." He pursed his lips, pretending to give the other name his full consideration. "Ninny . . . I am not so sure."

She gave a fleeting smile, pressing her fingers quickly to her lips, to prevent the movement opening the split at the corner of her mouth.

"Sorry about that one. Perhaps we had better dispense with that in favour of the other?"

Leif nodded, smiling. "I think so."

He insisted on sitting her back in the car while he fed the hens.

"I must hurry," he told her. "If we are a long time, the police and the doctor may arrive before we're back."

Kirsty blinked. "But we haven't called them yet."

Leif reached across, indicating the telephone lying on the dashboard. "I called from here, when I fetched the goats. I shall not be happy until that man is in custody."

He was not long away. Kirsty sat anxiously in the front passenger seat, painfully aware — now that the first shock had passed — that the upholstery of his luxurious Bentley was mud-streaked from contact with her clothes. Why did it always have to be like this? Why couldn't he have seen her looking reasonably attractive, for once?

She was dabbing at her eyes with his handkerchief when he returned.

"I'm sorry, Leif — your beautiful car."

He snorted. "Is a car, Kirsty. You are a person."

Kirsty sniffed. "A stupid person. All that looking over my shoulder, not to mention the carefully arranged telephone calls, and when he comes I go and fall for the oldest trick in the world."

★ ★ ★

Leif frowned, slid from his seat to close the gate behind them, and eased himself back again.

"Looking over your shoulder? Telephone calls? You are saying that you have known this man is coming? He is not a stranger to you?"

205

"I've never seen him before," she hastened to explain, "but I know who he is." Quickly she outlined the circumstances.

Leif glanced at her, then quickly turned his eyes back to the road. "Yet you had no protection?"

"Sarah rang at five, Jenny at six, Sergeant Ryan at seven," she told him. "After that I locked myself in."

"But your nearest neighbour is afforded no knowledge of the fact." He spoke quietly, seeming hurt.

"Sarah said I should tell you," Kirsty admitted honestly. "I did consider it, but I thought it sounded so stupid to ask for protection from a man I didn't know, and who might never arrive. I told her you'd think I was mad."

A wry smile came to his lips, but he said nothing. They were now in sight of the Volvo, but it was no longer alone on the road. Two police cars, strategically placed alongside and behind, partly obscured it from view.

As the Bentley drew up beside Sergeant Ryan's vehicle, two burly constables emerged from the other police car. Leif handed them the keys and rotor arm, which he had removed from the Volvo.

"I'll go and collect the pick-up." Kirsty unfastened her seat belt. "Thank you for all you've done, Leif. I'll return your handkerchief tomorrow." She put her hand on the door catch.

Leif reached across, holding it closed.

"I do not bring you here simply to collect your pick-up. It's not fit for you to be alone tonight, Kirsty. You will stay at Tall Trees."

Kirsty blinked. "You're very kind, but really it's not necessary. I'll go to bed as soon as I've seen the doctor, and . . . "

"Yes." Calmly Leif re-fastened her seat belt. "Robbie has already prepared the bed, and I have no doubt that the doctor will agree that it's the best plan."

"I agree, too, Miss." Sergeant Ryan spoke through the open window. "These weeks on your own up here are bound to have been a strain, and now you've had a bad shock. Best have company tonight, eh?"

In the face of their closed ranks, Kirsty was forced to capitulate. It was true that she had no desire to be alone.

A short lapse in the conversation was enough to allow pictures of the man's threatening face back into her mind. There was no doubt that, if she could relax at all in the loneliness of Refuge Farm, her sleep would be shattered by nightmares.

"Are the keys in the pick-up, Miss?" Sergeant Ryan was moving off towards the front of the Bentley. "I'll lock it up for you. Is there anything you need out of it?"

Kirsty nodded gratefully. "Just my bag, please, from the passenger seat."

Passing it through the window, a few minutes later, he smiled kindly. "I'll be following you up in a little while, Miss, to take a statement."

As Leif drew the Bentley to a smooth halt outside Tall Trees, Robbie came hurrying down the steps.

"Oh, my poor dear. How dreadful. Come along in. I have a warm drink waiting, and a bed prepared."

Kirsty glanced at Leif, who nodded. "Go with Robbie. I shall put the car in the garage, and be in directly. Ah!" His eye travelled to another vehicle, just pulling into the yard. "Here is the doctor."

Robbie led the way up the wide staircase to the cosy guest room, between Leif's bedroom and Minna's. A pilot light, on the switch below the delicately carved bedside table, indicated an electric blanket warming the bed. Spread on the blue silk eiderdown was a fine cotton nightdress.

"It will be far too big, my dear, but it was the best I could do at short notice." Robbie apologised, holding it against Kirsty. "Now you pop into bed, and I'll bring the doctor up in a few minutes."

The bed was deliciously warm and soft. Kirsty began to feel drowsy the moment she laid her head on the pillow.

Dr. Taylor was as gentle in his examination of her, as he had been with Timothy. He tended to her wounds, strapped up her ribs, then began to mix something in a small glass.

"I'm giving you a mild sedative," he told her, smiling at her expression. "Yes, I know you're sleepy already, but you need to relax completely."

Afterwards, Kirsty remembered his leaving the room, but little else other than vague impressions: Robbie, placing a drink on the table, a fleeting glimpse of Sergeant Ryan, Leif, still and silent, gazing down at her — then, perhaps at a later time, tucking her hand under the covers. Scenes which remained unregistered in her mind until she woke completely, hours later, in the middle of the night.

Her first feeling, as her eyes flicked open, was one of bewilderment at her strange surroundings. Relief followed in a moment. Of course. The guest room at Tall Trees. Protected, safe, she was among friends. The sedative had worn off. She no longer felt sleepy, just warm and comfortable.

Kirsty glanced round the room. Lined velvet curtains, deep pile carpet. How spartan her bedroom at Refuge would seem after this.

She allowed her eyelids to droop. Sunday tomorrow. If she felt well enough, she would visit Timothy at Westfield. The necessity for secrecy had passed. He might even come back to Refuge to stay.

On the edge of sleep, a sound filtered into her mind. A child crying. She must go and give comfort. It was most unusual for Timothy to wake and . . . No, that was wrong. How confused her thoughts were. Timothy was not here at Tall Trees. The sobbing child must be Minna!

5

SUDDENLY, she was fully awake, turning back the covers, sliding to the floor. Out of the cocoon of blankets, the night air felt chill, but she paid no heed. The child was whimpering piteously. She must go to her.

No sound came from any other room as she glided swiftly along the softly-lit passage to Minna's door. There she stopped, listening intently. It was all right. No one else was with the child. She wouldn't be intruding by going in.

"Make him go away. Make him go away."

Minna buried her face into her shoulder, as Kirsty sat on the bed, winding her arms round her.

"Hush," Kirsty held the trembling little body gently. "There's no one here but me. You've had a bad dream, that's all."

Minna clung tightly to her arms. "Can we have the light on, Kirsty?"

Kirsty stroked the bright hair back

from the little girl's puckered face. "All right. Then you'll see that there's nothing to be afraid of."

Reaching out a hand, she pushed the switch on the small bedside lamp. "Oh, that's a pretty light, Minna." She ran a finger down the side. "It's like a candle, isn't it?"

Minna nodded.

"There's a song about a candle." Kirsty told her. "Do you know it?"

The little girl shook her head.

"Would you like me to sing it to you?"

A faint smile. "Yes."

"Well, it goes like this." She began to sing softly, in her sweet voice. "Jesus bids us shine with a clear, pure light. Like a little candle burning in the night." She indicated the bedside light. "In this land of darkness, we must shine. You in your small corner, and I in mine." She brushed a kiss on the smooth cheek. "There, do you like that song?"

Minna nodded. "Please will you sing it again?"

Kirsty laughed. "Just once more, then." As she went through the song again, she lowered the little girl to the pillow. "Now

I think it's time we all stopped shining and went to sleep again." She reached for the light switch.

"Can't I keep it on, Kirsty, please!"

"Well," Kirsty hesitated, "it isn't really for me to say, love."

"Why?" Minna's blue eyes stared up at her. "You're a lady, aren't you?"

"I hope so. I expect you really mean 'grown up', but that doesn't mean that I can give permission for anything in someone else's house. It's impolite for a guest to do that. The host should be the one to decide."

Minna frowned. "What's a host?"

"The owner of the house," Kirsty explained.

The little girl smiled. "Min farbror."

"That's right." Kirsty nodded. "However, in this case, I think it will be all right." She folded the cover back, tucking it in at the side. "Come on now, head down or you're going to be one very sleepy little girl in the morning."

Minna smiled sleepily. "Night, Kirsty." Then she looked past her, towards the door, "Night, Farbror Leif."

Kirsty turned swiftly. Long bronzed

214

legs protruding from his black cotton robe, Leif leaned, arms folded, in the doorway. Smiling, he came forward.

"Ah, so the guest has not entirely usurped the position of the host." Clearly he had been there long enough to hear most of the conversation.

Coming up beside her, he bent over Minna. "Do I rate a kiss, too?"

Minna flung her arms round his neck, hugging him tightly as she gave him a kiss. He laughed softly, hugging her back, before gently replacing her on the pillow. "All right, now?"

"Yes, thank you." As Minna's eyes sparkled up at him, Kirsty slipped out of the door. The child's words, in Leif's native tongue, illustrated so clearly the bond between father and daughter.

She sighed. Panic over. Back to bed, Kirsty, and leave them together. Closing her bedroom door, she slid between the covers, rubbing her feet to warm them 'You might wish you were part of their world, but face the fact that you're not. You'll be away back at Refuge tomorrow . . . and tomorrow . . . and tomorrow,' she told herself.

"Kirsty?" Startled out of her thoughts by the knock on her door, she leaned up on one elbow.

"Come in, Leif."

He seemed to fill the small room.

"I'm sorry that Minna has disturbed your sleep."

"Oh, she didn't," Kirsty hastened to reassure him. "I was awake already."

"You are unable to sleep? You are not comfortable?"

Kirsty laughed. "You must be joking. After all this luxury, I fear that I shall never sleep again at Refuge. Here, I could sleep for a week."

"Good." He smiled. "It's Sunday tomorrow. A day of rest."

"Mm." She nodded. "I was thinking of going to see Timothy."

His smile broadened. "Yes, we'll take Minna."

"You mean you'll come with me?" Kirsty's eyes were wide.

Leif nodded. "I should like to see the boy. Is all right?"

"Oh yes," she assured him. "He'll be so pleased to see you. Thank you."

He smiled. "Now it is time to rest or

216

you are perhaps one very sleepy little girl in the morning."

He had copied her words to Minna, yet somehow instilled into them more meaning.

Kirsty laughed. "You could be right."

★ ★ ★

She woke late. There was no sound from the other rooms upstairs, as she hastily washed, and combed her long hair.

Downstairs, she crept shamefaced into the kitchen to find Leif, alone, pouring coffee.

"I was going to bring it up to you," he complained.

Kirsty looked round. "Where is everyone?"

Smiling, he placed one normal-sized, and one small mug on a tray.

"We are the only two up this morning."

"At this time?" Kirsty glanced at the clock. "Goodness I must fly. I'm an hour late for the goats."

"But I am not." Leif's expression was serious, yet his eyes twinkled.

As she blinked at him, uncomprehending, he boasted. "Your goats are

217

fed and milked. The hens, too."

Kirsty grinned. "Milked?"

He picked up the tray, crossing the room to the door. "That sounds more like the Kirsty I am used to." In the doorway, he turned, frowning, giving his head a little shake. "You still do not look like her."

She touched the corner of her mouth, ruefully. "So bad, is it? I hoped it wasn't too noticeable this morning."

"I do not mean the bruising, Kirsty."

She frowned. "Then what?"

"You are so . . . feminine. I do not imagine . . . or the long hair."

He did not imagine what, or the long hair? Deciding not to press the matter, Kirsty's eyes danced.

"You expected me to be solidly built, with a crew cut, didn't you?"

He hesitated. "I thought your hair would be short style."

She made a face. "Sorry to disappoint you."

He shook his head. "It's no disappointment. It's a pleasure to look at."

Surprised by the sudden compliment, Kirsty gave a shy smile. "Thank you."

Further reflection bringing them to the decision that a morning visit to Westfield would upset Jenny's routine, they delayed their journey to Westfield until after lunch.

Kirsty's tentative suggestion that she should walk down to the pick-up, return to Refuge, and be picked up from there at the appropriate time, was quickly put down by all three parties. Leif smugly replied that he had returned the pick-up to Refuge when he had gone down to milk the goats. Robbie took the view that Kirsty still needed to rest and, once at Refuge, would pitch straight into work. Minna just wanted her to stay.

Sunday morning at Tall Trees was a relaxed, happy time, Kirsty found. Seeing Leif playing with his little daughter, relaxing in his chair, reading the Sunday papers, it was difficult to remember that this was the tough, cool-headed businessman, head of a vast estate. It was even more difficult to reconcile herself to the fact that his attitude to her was mere kindness — he preferred the company of Leila Fennel.

This fact was illustrated only too clearly at around eleven-thirty that morning, when Robbie took a break from the lunch preparations to make coffee. Leif had taken a telephone call in the office and, persuaded by Robbie that it would be in order to take his drink in to him, Kirsty entered quietly.

Engrossed in his call, Leif didn't hear her enter, and before he took the precaution of silence, she had caught part of the conversation.

He was speaking in a low urgent tone. "We cannot, Leila. It's best for the child that she knows nothing of our true relationship. You must see that . . . "

Looking up at that point, he stopped speaking to smile warmly at Kirsty, but put his hand over the mouthpiece, and remained silent until she had left the room.

Had she been of a different temperament, Leif's intimate telephone conversation with Leila Fennel would have spoiled the remainder of her day. Kirsty, however, was well aware that the position which allowed her to have knowledge of the call was enviable in itself.

Robbie elected to have a quiet afternoon at home, so it was a party of three — Leif, Kirsty and Minna — who set out in the Bentley. A quick stop at Refuge for Kirsty to change into clean clothes, and they were on their way.

The conversation of both adults was mainly connected with the child, rather than between themselves, but Leif seemed in particularly good spirits, humming snatches of a catchy little tune at intervals.

Timothy was in the yard, bouncing a ball against the wall. Seeing the Bentley, he stopped, stared at Kirsty stepping out, then came whooping as she was followed by Leif and Minna.

"Miss, you've brought Mr. A."

Kirsty laughed. "In point of fact, it's the other way round. How are you today?"

"Lots better, Miss, but I can go to school tomorrow."

The peeved tone brought another smile to Kirsty's face. "'But' I can go to school?" she queried. "I should have thought you'd be bored after all this time."

"Not me, Miss." Timothy shook his head. "I wouldn't care if . . . " He stopped, peering at Kirsty. "What happened to you, Miss?"

"Walked into a door," said Kirsty promptly.

"Go on! Expect me to believe that? Somebody's 'ad a go at you, 'aven't they?" Pulling himself up straight, he gave a sudden belligerent movement towards Leif. "Was it 'im, Miss?"

"It was not!" Leif exploded.

Kirsty laughed. "Do you think I would be with him now, if it was?"

Timothy relaxed. "Nah, you got more sense'n that."

She raised her eyebrows. "Thank you for those few kind words."

"Hey up, you two," Jenny hailed them from outside the furthest goat house and, as they turned towards her, Timothy caught Minna's hand.

"Come on, kid, got somefink to tell yer."

"He is more tolerant of girls than most boys of his age." Leif smiled, as they strolled across the yard towards Jenny.

"Mm." Kirsty frowned.

"You do not approve?"

She laughed. "I'm suspicious. I'm suspicious of anything connected with young Master Hurst. There's usually an ulterior motive to his actions, especially when he's at his most affable. Did you notice his exact words?"

Leif shrugged. "No, I didn't."

"He said 'I have something to tell you' — not something to show you. Show would make it a necessity to take her wherever it was. 'Tell' could mean that whatever he had to say was not for our ears."

"What will happen to the boy?" Leif was suddenly serious.

Kirsty sighed. "He'll be kept in care — other than that, I don't know."

"He will not go back to his mother?"

She shook her head. "I doubt it. She's married this one, you see."

He raised his eyebrows. "There have been others?"

Kirsty snorted. "Quite a procession."

★ ★ ★

223

Leif opened the wire gate to the field, allowed her through, and closed it after them. "She is an attractive woman?"

She looked up, eyes flicking over his face, appraising him.

"Not to you, I wouldn't think."

"Why's that?"

She laughed. "Why? I would imagine you'd have better taste."

He made a face. "A compliment. Thank you."

"Not much of one, I'm afraid." Seeing his quizzical expression, she added, "Timothy's mother is a bleached blonde, with a vocabulary that would make you blush, and a figure second only to my Aunt Lydia."

He nodded. "I see — and the men?"

"Put in a line, they'd look like a reunion from some prison."

He exploded into laughter, and she grinned.

"There! I told you I'd make you laugh one day. The funniest part is, this happens to be true. Petty criminals, drunks, drug addicts — she can certainly pick them. I suspect that she only married this one because he had money."

They walked for a few yards in silence. Then she said. "It's Timothy's review soon. I expect they'll decide then."

"Review?" Clearly he was puzzled.

"Every so often they review the case of a child in care, and make recommendations as to its future. He may be put out for adoption, I suppose, if his mother agrees."

"You will adopt him, Kirsty?"

Kirsty shook her head. "I can't afford it. It sounds mercenary, I know, but it's an unfortunate fact that without the weekly cheque, I could never manage to keep him." She sighed. "Anyway, it's just as well. He's a man's boy. The one thing he really needs is something I can't give him — a father."

"I'll second that." Hobbling up to them on her crutches, Jenny said, "Had the stuffing knocked out of him when he first came, but now he's keeping me going, I can tell you. Whatever he'll be up to next doesn't bear thinking about." She turned to Kirsty. "You'll be taking him back with you?"

Kirsty looked up at Leif, hopefully. "Could we?"

He nodded. "Of course, if you . . . "

"Mr. A! Mr. A!" As Timothy shouted, Leif broke his sentence, turning towards him. "That thing in your car is buzzing, Mr. A."

"The telephone," Leif explained. "Sorry. I'll be back directly."

He was — quickly and apologetically. "I have to leave now. Forgive me, but I am needed elsewhere. The boy's clothes are packed?"

"All packed and ready to go." Jenny wiped her hands on her hessian apron. "But you'll be having a cuppa with us before you go?"

"I'm afraid I haven't the time," Leif apologised. "Kirsty may stay, of course, if she so wishes, but I must take Minna with me."

"No. Thanks all the same, Jenny, but we'll go with Leif," Kirsty decided at once. "It will be far easier in the long run."

The quick proposal was put forward to cover her disappointment. A moment ago it had been such an enjoyable afternoon. How suddenly it had changed. Leif couldn't wait to be on his way.

Dispirited, she allowed Leif to carry Timothy's luggage into the kitchen at Refuge, and followed him back to the gate. Before they reached it, he turned, speaking in a low voice so that Minna could not hear.

"I intend to ask you, Kirsty. Soon is Minna's birthday. We have a party. A surprise for her. You will come, ja? You — and the boy?"

Kirsty's eyes sparkled. "I'd love to — we'd love to. Thank you. When is it to be?"

He smiled. "Saturday. Six days from today."

The thought of the party kept Kirsty in the brightest of spirits for the next few days. So what if Leila Fennel would be there, too? Leif cared enough to invite her. Maybe it was just for Minna — maybe not. The point was that she would be there in his house as a guest, for a second time.

When she received the telephone call from Sarah, imparting the news that Timothy's review had been fixed for the Friday, and they would need to travel to town, she was pleased. The review was to be on the day before Minna's party, and she would be able to buy her present in town.

Throughout the week she had no contact with Leif, other than the few moments, morning and evening, when he collected and dropped Timothy. Even then they had little conversation, since Leif seemed not disposed to take time enough to make any. It did not dampen Kirsty's sparkling mood.

Robbie spent Thursday afternoon sorting out dishes for the spread, to be prepared the next day. Kirsty would have liked to be there, assisting in the preparation — putting her skills into practice with dozens of appetising delights; instead, she spent the entire train journey describing them to Timothy.

"It will be an enormous buffet meal," she explained, "traditional in Norway. You start at one end, and progress down. There is herring and seafood and salad, sliced meat, scrambled eggs, meat balls, sausages, fried potatoes. Too much . . ." she laughed . . . "even for you to get through it all."

They spent hours trying to locate a

kaleidoscope — which Kirsty had set her mind on, as a suitable present for the little girl — and their arrival back at Refuge was much later than was their intention.

The review — supposedly the main reason for their journey — had taken the least time of all. In the space of half-an-hour, his notes had been read, the boy interviewed, and the decision taken to take steps towards 'a more permanent arrangement'. Even Kirsty's chat to her old friend Sarah took longer — particularly as she had some amazing news.

"I'm going to marry Monty."

"You're joking, Sarah."

Her friend had laughed. "I knew you'd say that, but I'm not, you know. I'm deadly serious, Kirsty. I'm sick and tired of sorting out other people's problems, of worrying myself into old age about things which I, and nobody else, can change. I want a bit of luxury in my life, and I intend to get it. Monty asked me, and I accepted — so that's that. Nothing more to be said."

Except congratulations. Stammered

words, which did not — could not — spring from Kirsty's heart when, knowing Monty, with every fibre of her being she felt that it was a complete mistake.

* * *

From the moment she rose on the Saturday morning, Kirsty worked with one eye on the clock. She was going to dress up for this party, and give herself time to make absolutely sure of looking her best.

It was a gorgeous day. The sun streamed from the bluest of blue skies as Timothy, resplendent in shirt and tie, hair neatly brushed, and shoes that Kirsty could see her face in — stepped out of the door, to where Kirsty waited by the newly-washed and polished pick-up.

He looked Kirsty up and down, a wide grin spreading over his pale features. "Cor, you look ace, Miss. After 'im, ain't yer?"

There was no answer to that — mainly because it was true. Kirsty had chosen her best outfit, and made herself ready with extreme care.

The result was more striking than she would have imagined. Bought for her end-of-college dance, and worn only on the one occasion, the white cotton dress set off her long, shining hair to perfection.

Kirsty had taken the hair back from either side off her head to fasten with slides, revealing the delicate structure of her face.

Stepping carefully over the gravel in her white sandals, Kirsty slid into the pick-up beside Timothy. "All set, young man? Clean handkerchief in pocket, and best behaviour uppermost?"

"You bet, Miss."

"Then off we go!"

She kept to a slow pace all the way to Tall Trees. Timothy was on the edge of his seat the whole time, causing her to glance anxiously at his seat-belt, hoping that it was properly fastened. It was with a sense of relief that Kirsty turned into the forecourt of Tall Trees, and pulled up almost at the bottom of the steps leading to the door. Almost, because directly in front of the doorway stood Leila Fennel's sports car.

"Beaten us to it." She grinned at Timothy, nodding towards it. "Never mind. Come on. They say if you can't beat them, join them."

Laughing together, they stepped out of the pick-up — relaxed, happy, and completely unaware that anything was amiss, until Leila slid silkily out of her own vehicle, and confronted them.

"I'm so glad I came, Miss Trensham. Leif said there was no need, but I told him that you're not as used to his whims as I am. She hardly knows you, I said. What if she takes you at your word, my darling, and comes to a party that doesn't exist?"

"Doesn't exist?" Kirsty's face paled. A quick glance at Timothy revealed him open-mouthed and motionless, obviously at as much of a loss to understand as she was herself. "I'm afraid I don't understand, Miss Fennel. Where is everyone?"

"Gone." Gone, too, were the silky-sweet tones that Leila had employed at the start of the conversation. Now she emerged haughtily triumphant.

"Gone?" Kirsty echoed blankly. "Gone where?"

"To Norway, of course. To celebrate the birthday with the grandparents." Irritably, Leila drew back an elegant black glove to consult the slim gold watch round her wrist. Clearly the game was beginning to pall.

"Naturally, I am to join them. My flight is in a few hours. I have to go."

"But," Kirsty stammered, unable to believe that this was really happening, "But why?" Hadn't she, only the day before yesterday, gone over all the arrangements and menu with Robbie, in this very house?"

"Because I'm invited — why do you think?"

"I mean, why has everyone gone to Norway? The party was arranged here. I discussed it all with Robbie. It doesn't make sense."

"It would make sense if you really knew Leif Amundsen, as I do." The attitude had changed again to a patronising kindness. "You mustn't rely on him, my dear. A sudden whim and he'll change his

233

mind and leave you flat — as he appears to have done on this occasion."

* * *

Kirsty flushed, but said nothing. Utterly deflated, she dare not trust herself to speak, lest her voice tremble and give indication of her shattering disappointment. It must be true. Had the family been at home, Robbie would have been out here by now to welcome them in. Minna would be flying down the steps in party dress calling, "Come and see, Kirsty, come and see." Even Leif — but, no. She wasn't going to think about Leif. Not ever again. How could he do this to her? How could he do it to Timothy, who had already been through so much?

"Miss Trensham!"

Slipping a comforting arm round Timothy's shoulders, Kirsty forced herself to speak in a calm, friendly tone. She even managed a smile.

"Yes, Miss Fennel?"

"I said there will be no need for you to clean the house while Mr. Amundsen and party are away. I will keep the keys with me, and it will remain locked."

Kirsty nodded respectfully. "Of course, Miss Fennel, I understand."

It was a pity that there would ever be need to clean his house again. To go off — both he and Robbie — without a word, a note, anything to explain. If she had not given her solemn promise to work for him indefinitely, this most certainly would be the last time that she ever set foot on a square inch of ground belonging to Leif Amundsen.

Leila was about to close the car door, when Kirsty held forward the gaily-wrapped parcel. "Perhaps you would be good enough to give this to Minna, with my best wishes?"

Leila blinked, staring from the parcel to Kirsty with an odd, almost alarmed, expression. Then she recovered. "Certainly, Miss Trensham. Though I expect the child will be inundated with handsome gifts."

'Meaning that ours isn't good enough,' thought Kirsty. The moment that the sleek sports car had pulled out of sight, she turned to Timothy. "Tim, I'm so sorry. What can I say, I . . . " She stopped, appalled.

Silently, motionless, the child was crying. Tears were running down his face unchecked, as an adult cries in disbelief and despair.

Gently, she hugged him against her. "I know, my love, I know. I'm disappointed, too, but never mind. Look, it's a super day. Let's go home and get changed, and we'll go for a picnic by the river. How does that sound?"

The boy nodded and, fishing his handkerchief from his pocket, Kirsty handed it to him. "Come on, love, have a good blow."

"Yes, Miss."

Guiding him to the pick-up, Kirsty knew that it was not enough. The boy's grief was not merely for a lost party — it was for an idol. Leif Amundsen had somehow become the central figure in their world. He had let them down badly. So much for his honour and dependability.

Although the trip to the river bank could not be called a success, it filled the blank afternoon. Normally both Timothy and Kirsty would have been delighted with the antics of the squirrels in the trees at the far side of the river. Today they viewed them as possessions of their unreliable neighbour.

Most of the food was re-loaded into the basket and brought home. Looking forward to the delicacies at Tall Trees, the goat cheese sandwiches seemed dull and unappetising.

Kirsty had planned nothing for the Sunday. She had expected that, after the excitement of the party, a time of rest and simple fare would be in order. Now she felt obliged to come up with something to pass the time, so taking Timothy's mind away from his disappointment.

The answer came during their morning walk in the wood. Coming across a huge bank of foxgloves already in bud, Kirsty decided that they were just what they needed to brighten up the entrance to Refuge Farm.

On either side of the gate, Timothy dug two narrow beds, and planted the flowers while Kirsty collected small white pebbles to place along the edge.

Their pleasure in their task made

them hungry, and they found themselves devouring with relish the same food that they had despised on the river bank the day before.

On Monday morning, Kirsty watered the new flower beds before the sun was up. If the foxgloves flagged, Timothy would be disappointed after all his hard work.

It seemed a strange, long day. Having become used to spending much of her time at Tall Trees, it seemed odd to be working in her own house on a weekday, and lonely to have no one with whom to exchange the odd word. By the time evening came, she was glad to be occupied with organising, and listening to, Timothy's mountain of homework.

It was just after eight o'clock when the telephone rang the next morning. Already the goats were milked, the hens fed, and Kirsty was just setting out Timothy's breakfast.

"Kirsty Trensham."

She was unprepared for the familar voice, or its casual tone.

"Leif here. I returned home late last

night. Minna is not at school today, but I have to go into the village. I will take the boy for you."

It took all her effort to answer with any degree of politeness.

"Thank you, Mr. Amundsen, but it won't be necessary. I'll deliver and collect Timothy myself from now on."

"Why?" She could almost see the frown.

"Why? Well, I think it's best not to rely on other people in future."

"You think I am unreliable?"

"Yes, Mr. Amundsen." She spoke calmly and deliberately. "As a matter of fact, I do. I believe I have every reason to think so."

"I do not." His tone was curt.

"You wouldn't, would you? Only someone who has spent half their life in a children's home could appreciate how much even a simple occasion, like a birthday party, could mean to a boy like Timothy. He cried, Mr. Amundsen, do you know that? He's had a hard life, and he's a tough little chap; it takes a lot to upset him. Watching him, I could have wept, too. I think that, if you didn't

239

mean to keep your word, it would have been better not to extend the invitation at all."

"And I think," his voice was cold, "that I had better come to discuss this."

"There's nothing to discuss," she told him, "and I've no time now for idle chatter. Thank you for all you've done in that direction in the past, but I will manage the transportation myself in the future. Goodbye, Mr. Amundsen."

"Kirsty!" His voice came back so sharply that she jumped and nearly dropped the receiver. "I shall continue to call you Kirsty, no matter how you choose to address me. I have said that we need to talk, and I do not intend to be put off — now, or at any other time. I will see you in a few minutes."

And a few minutes it was. As she turned away from the telephone, Timothy was just starting on his cereal. He had only just cleared his plate when Leif's Range Rover screeched to a halt at the gate.

★ ★ ★

By the time Kirsty, followed by Timothy, got outside, Leif was already ushering a sleepy-looking Minna through the gate. With no preliminaries of greeting, he muttered in a low voice, "Send the children away, please. I wish to speak to you alone."

Kirsty turned to Timothy. "Just take Minna to see the guinea pigs for a little while, there's a good lad . . . "

"Now . . . " Leif faced her squarely, the moment the children had disappeared from view . . . "You will tell me what I have done to upset you."

Kirsty glared. "You know what you've done."

"You will tell me, please."

"All right," Kirsty raised her head defiantly, to look straight into his eyes. "You decided, after all our arrangements, to take Minna to Norway to spend her birthday with her grandparents."

Once it was out, she flushed, and could no longer look at him. How stupid it sounded when she actually voiced her complaint. What a childish attitude, to confront her neighbour in anger about something that was quite understandable — even a good idea. Only it had not seemed like that at the time.

"Decided?" Hooking his thumbs in his belt, he marched a few steps away from her, then, breathing hard, he rounded on her again. "Decided? You make it sound like a . . . a . . . " he circled a hand as if conjuring a word . . . "notion . . . a fancy to take a few days of holiday."

"Wasn't it?"

He glared. "You think that is in my character to be so unpredictable?"

Kirsty shrugged. "I wouldn't know. Miss Fennel said it was."

"Miss Fennel!" Leif fairly spat the word. "So you take her word before mine?"

"You gave me no word," Kirsty answered haughtily. "You told me nothing."

"Because you were not here!"

There was a moment of silence, then Kirsty said quietly. "It was Timothy's review day. I had told you about it. You knew where I was."

"But I couldn't get hold of you to give you a message before I go — and it would seem that Leila did not fulfill her promise to do so." He turned away, then turned sharply back again. "Can you not see that Leila is a spiteful, jealous woman, who would go to any lengths to further her own ends?"

Kirsty said nothing. She could believe that. She wanted to believe it all, but . . .

"You say the boy cried." Leif began to speak again in an agitated fashion. "For that I am sorry — but I cried, too, that day."

"You?" Kirsty stared.

Clapping a huge hand to his chest, the fingers spread wide, he leaned towards her. "I, too, am capable of emotion. But I do not cry for a stupid party," he said with sincerity.

He dropped his hand, hooking his thumb back on his belt, his chest heaving. "I cry for something that is lost to me forever. For my friend who shared my college days — the studies, the hopes and dreams of our future." He stopped for a moment, to take two or three long, deep breaths, then went on. "All I can do is stand there in silence. All I can think is that my friend Robin is dead. No more will he play a joke on me.

All these years since the accident, his mind is trapped in a useless body. He is frustrated and angry — so am I — but always there is hope. Now there is none, and my responsibilities seem suddenly too heavy."

Turning suddenly away, he leaned on the gatepost, burying his head on his arm. "I have had enough!"

★ ★ ★

Kirsty was appalled. She had been completely taken in by Leila Fennel's explanation, when all the time he was going through this dreadful experience.

Quickly, she stepped forward. "I'm so very sorry, Leif."

Her voice came softly and, as her gentle hand touched his sleeve, he turned swiftly, snatching her into his arms, his chest heaving as he buried his face in her soft hair.

But hardly had she closed her own comforting arms about him than a piercing shriek shattered their new-found trust, ripping them apart — Leif to stand, head bowed, hand on the gate, his back

244

turned. Kirsty to run towards the sound, catching the child as she hurtled through the door.

"Minna! What is it — what's happened?"

The little girl clutched at Kirsty, burying her head against her shoulder. "It's a bee! It's a bee!"

"Oh, is that all?" Kirsty sighed with relief. "There's no need to be frightened of a bee. She's not going to hurt you."

Minna blinked. "She?"

"Certainly." Kirsty nodded. "That's a worker bee, and the workers are all ladies — well, they would be, wouldn't they?"

Straightening up, she took the little girl's hand, and led her towards the new flower beds at the gate, lifting her so that she could see over the wall.

"Now you watch. She's far too busy to go round stinging people. The only reason she came buzzing round you is that you look so pretty, and smell so nice, that she thought you were a flower."

Minna giggled. "A flower?"

"That's right." Kirsty smiled. "And it's her job to go round all the flowers, collecting the sweet, sticky nectar."

Minna looked from the bee to Kirsty. "Does she eat it?"

Kirsty shook her head. "No. She collects as much as she can carry, then takes it back to the hive where she lives. There she and lots of other lady bees build honeycombs, and turn the nectar into honey to feed the baby bees, and the queen bee — and the lazy old drones, who do not work at all. They're the men."

"Ahem!" An exaggerated cough made Kirsty look up, to find Leif, smiling now, indicating his watch.

She made a face at Minna. "Oh dear. Here's one man who likes to work, and we're keeping him from it."

Lifting her from the wall, she took the child's hand and led her to the gate, where Leif was waiting. "Sorry."

He laughed. "It's just that I prefer to have the boy there on time, even if he does not!"

His expressive glance over her shoulder made Kirsty turn, to see Timothy dawdling along, dragging his school bag.

"Come on, my lad," she called. "Mr. Amundsen has more to do than wait for you, you know." She turned to Leif. "I'll be up about ten o'clock, if that's all right?"

"Up?" Leif looked puzzled.

"To your house," she reminded him. "I'm still an employee, you know."

"Of course." He raised his head in pretended arrogance. "I forget that I have a slave. But . . . " fishing under his jacket, he removed a key from his belt . . . "you will need this to get in, Kirsty, in case I'm not yet home."

Kirsty blinked. "Isn't Robbie there?"

"No." He shook his head. "I left her in Norway. She needs to rest — so does my mother." He gave a sudden smile. "Neither of them take kindly to it. Together they will chat — not notice so much the passing of time."

"But how will you manage without her?"

He shrugged. "Easily." Then again he smiled, adding, "Provided I can count on your help?"

Watching him go with the children, Kirsty felt a thrill of excitement. The new arrangements would put her virtually in sole charge. There could be occasional

247

meals together, and . . .

There she went again, reading romance into perfectly ordinary situations. All he's interested in is a reasonably good-tempered person to help look after the child. Meals together simply will not materialise. Keep your mind on the house, and off its master, and the arrangement will work out fine.

It did. The labour-saving devices at Tall Trees made it an easy house to manage, and menus for two people she could devise in plenty. Keeping an outward appearance of calm serenity, Kirsty was loving with the child, friendly and reliable towards the father — who began to show his gratitude in ways which could have been interpreted quite differently, had Kirsty allowed her mind to fly in that direction, which she didn't.

Consistently she told herself that his little gifts were given in simple appreciation of her efforts: small tokens of thanks for a job well done. It did not detract from the pleasure of receiving. The new brand of chocolates that he thought she might like to try; the small illustrated book of wild plants that he spotted on a shelf; the lovely bunch of freshly gathered flowers, which appeared on the seat of the pick-up, with no word at all. Each gave her much greater pleasure than Kirsty would have cared to admit.

It was two weeks after Leif had returned from Norway that this divine existence came to a sudden end. Leif had gone to collect the children from school, and Kirsty was in the stable at Refuge, when a vehicle stopped at the gate.

Thinking that it was Leif returning, she stuck her head round the door to find herself confronted by a stranger. A stocky sandy-haired man, he came forward, holding out his hand. "Miss Trensham, I believe?"

Kirsty nodded, puzzled. "That's right."

A bright smile broke over the freckled face. "Brian Hurst. Very pleased to meet you."

Kirsty frowned. "Should I know you?"

The smile broadened. "No, but this letter will explain who I am."

Taking the note, Kirsty scanned it with growing incredulity.

"You are Timothy's father?"

"So I'm given to understand. I must admit that the idea is very new to me. Until a short time ago, I had no notion of his existence."

Kirsty took a deep breath, trying to come to terms with the news.

"I think we had better go inside, and you can tell me all about it."

For the next ten minutes, Kirsty sat enthralled by a story that seemed equivalent to a fairy tale. She had always supposed that Timothy's father had deserted his mother. It transpired that it was the other way round.

A check of the dates had revealed that his wife was already pregnant when she left him. He had no knowledge of the fact, and throughout his search for her, and subsequent divorce, he had been given no indication that the child existed.

Five years ago, Brian Hurst had remarried; two years ago had been blessed with a bonny daughter. His wife, revealed in his photographs as a plump, rosy-cheeked, lady, had experienced a surprisingly difficult birth — so much so, that doctors advised against a second child. The idea of adoption gradually evolved, and it was sheer chance that, in the process, Brian Hurst had come to learn of his own son.

"The only thing is, Miss Trensham . . ." he gazed at her earnestly, "I want the boy to like me of his own accord, not feel obligated because I'm his father. I thought, if you wouldn't mind, I could be introduced as 'Uncle Brian', as if I was a friend of yours. I'm staying in Malton for a couple of weeks, so if I came over every day and let him get to know me, we would be able to tell if it was going to work out. Otherwise, he might be keen at first, because of who I am, and not really get along with me at all."

Kirsty thought it a very sensible idea, provided she could get the authorities to verify this man's story.

They were crossing the yard, laughing together at thoughts of Timothy's face when all was revealed, when the Range Rover arrived outside.

Unfurling himself from the seat, Leif lifted down first Minna, then a parcel. "Kirsty, it's stupid for us to go on . . ."

He saw Brian Hurst, and hesitated. "Sorry, I didn't realise that you had company."

His eyes were flicking over the man, taking in every detail.

"Er, yes," Kirsty stammered, flushing slightly. "I'm sorry . . . "

"No matter. You are ready, Minna?" He lifted the little girl up.

"So this is the boy?" Kirsty became aware that Brian Hurst was speaking.

"Yes, this is Timothy. Timothy, this is . . . er . . . Uncle Brian."

From the window of the Range Rover, Leif stared from Timothy's father to Kirsty, as she made the introduction, then, with no wave of the hand, and not another word, he drove away.

6

THE next day she was at Tall Trees early. Leif was in the habit of coming into the house for a coffee, on his return from school. If she had the drink ready, there would be a longer time to tell her story.

She watched from the window as the Range Rover pulled under the shed. Might as well pour it out — he would be in directly.

Treading the path from the window to the fast-cooling drinks, it took a full ten minutes for her to realise that he was not coming. Kirsty replaced the coffee in the pot. Not to worry. She could occupy herself very well until he came in at lunchtime.

If he came. Twelve-thirty came and went. One o'clock. Two. He was not coming in to lunch, either. He was not coming at all.

At three-fifteen, seeing the Range Rover reversing from under the shed, she dashed to the door and down the steps, waving. Leif gave no sign of having seen her, as he drove across the yard.

It was too late. When he returned, Timothy and Minna would be there, not to mention 'Uncle Brian'.

All day he had not come near the house — even to eat. Had he been so upset by the appearance of her unexpected visitor? Somehow she must explain.

Sorting out a last-minute neck-washing problem around eight o'clock, she heard a rattle at the front door. Dropping the flannel in the washbasin, she flew downstairs and dragged open the door — in time to see the Bentley glide away from the gate. On the mat was an envelope.

Anxiously, she ripped it open and spread out the small piece of expensive notepaper, only to become more deflated than ever as she read:

'I expect you intended to ask for time away from work, to entertain your friend. Of course, it is granted. Take as long as you wish. I can manage. Perhaps you can provide transport for the boy to and from school for a while. Minna is with Leila. Leif.'

Kirsty burst into tears.

That day, up at Tall Trees, was like a carbon copy of the previous one. She cleaned an already spotless house, prepared meals which no one came to eat — and finally left a large note on the centre of the kitchen table.

"Dear Leif, thank you, but I do not need time off. I am not entertaining anyone. Please get in touch. Love, Kirsty."

The word 'love' was sandwiched between the last word of the message and her signature, making it clear that it had been added as an afterthought. Kirsty felt that it would not be detrimental; that it might even give added weight, since she had particularly sought to include it.

In fact it made no difference either way. The note was still on the table the following morning, and when, throughout the day, it became clear that the only person going in and out of Tall Trees was herself, she decided to speak to Harry Carter.

The scream of the huge circular saw

deafened her, as she edged into the vast open-ended building. Nervous of going further, she waited until one of the men came near.

"Who were you wanting, love?" he shouted over the noise.

"I was looking for Harry Carter," she told him.

He looked surprised. "He's gone with gaffer, love."

"Oh," Kirsty made out that she understood. "I didn't know that he'd gone, too. No matter. I'll give Jenny a ring. Thanks very much."

★ ★ ★

How stupid she had been. Didn't Jenny always know what was going on? Back at Refuge, she went straight to the telephone.

"Jenny, where are Leif and Harry?"

"In Norway, looking over Leif's grandfather's place."

Kirsty gasped. "In Norway? So that's why I haven't seen him. But why has he left Minna — and with Leila, of all people?"

256

"If you mean why not with you, then you'll have to ask yourself that, young woman." Jenny was frank. "Probably left her because he thought she'd had enough time off school lately."

"Mm," Kirsty agreed. "That's true. I don't think she'll be very happy about it, though."

"You're right there. Late for school every morning, so Miss Pinder tells me."

"Oh, dear, is she?" Kirsty sighed. "When are they due back, do you know?"

"At the weekend, he said. Don't exactly know when."

Kirsty groaned. "Another day, at least. I wish he'd spoken to me before he went. Why are men so stubborn and unapproachable sometimes?"

"Wouldn't be men, if they weren't."

Kirsty laughed. "I suppose you're right. I'll just have to kick my heels for a while longer. Thanks, Jenny. Sorry I've kept you. No doubt you're extra busy with Harry away."

"Not with anything he could do," Jenny told her. "What do you think about some plain cheese and some chives, this year, for the garden party?"

"Sounds delicious. What garden party?"

"Church, on Saturday. O.K. That's what I'll do. Must get on. Time I was feeding up, and time you were fetching that young man."

Kirsty's eyes strayed to the clock. "Goodness, so it is. See you later, Jenny."

Rushing the call to a close, she flew outside to the pick-up. Three-twenty. Ten minutes before Timothy was due out of school. There was no telling what mischief he could be into, if she was not there at the gate.

As soon as she turned down the main street, Kirsty encountered mothers and children crowding the pavement. Parking the pick-up in the first available space, she grabbed the keys and ran the last twenty yards. No sign of a child at the gate. He wouldn't accept a lift from anyone, would he?

Reaching the gate, at last, she halted in astonishment. On the steps outside the door sat Timothy and Minna, hand in hand, forlorn and lost-looking.

Then they saw Kirsty. A whoop of joy, and both children hurtled across the playground to throw themselves into her arms.

"My goodness me, what's all this?" Kirsty laughed.

"We wondered where you was, Miss. You're always here when Mr. A's away," Timothy complained.

"Where you were," corrected Kirsty. "Sorry, I left it a bit late to set off."

"Am I coming with you?" Minna's blue eyes looked up hopefully.

"I don't think so, dear." Then, seeing the little face pucker, "But I'm not going to leave you. Come and sit on my knee in the pick-up, until somebody comes for you."

"Please can I stay with you?" In the cab, Minna tucked her head into Kirsty's shoulder.

"I'm sorry, darling." Kirsty hugged her. "There's nothing Tim and I would like better than to whisk you off home with us, but we haven't the right to do that."

"Are you a guest?" For a moment, Kirsty couldn't interpret the mumbled words. Then she laughed. Minna had remembered her lecture about the bedside light.

"It works the same way, Minna," she explained, gently. "You belong to your farbror, and he has left you in the care of Miss Fennel."

It was four-thirty before Leila Fennel's sports car appeared on the scene. There was no word of thanks, no apology, as Kirsty ushered the forlorn little girl into the passenger seat. Instead, Leila glared, slammed the door, and sped away without fastening Minna's safety belt.

Leif was right. A spiteful, jealous woman she was indeed.

The next morning, after dropping Timothy at the school gate, Kirsty followed one of the other young women across the road into the shop. It was unusually busy and, waiting at the back while the others present discussed their particular roles in Saturday's garden party, her eye lit on a display stand containing foreign phrase books.

Automatically Kirsty picked up the Norwegian one, flicking through the pages. Soon she was engrossed and contemplating buying the book. No, she decided. Where was the need to cultivate her knowledge of Norwegian? It didn't look as if there'd be any more friendly tête-à-têtes with Leif at this rate. She replaced the book.

"Let's hope the weather stays fine." The first customer was actually going. "See you tomorrow."

At last the shop cleared. As Kirsty eased her box of groceries round the door, allowing it to swing behind her, a screech of brakes made her look sharply to the road. To her horror, standing petrified in the middle, afraid to move either way, stood Minna.

"Stay there! I'll come and get you."

Dumping the box in the doorway, Kirsty ran to the trembling little girl, and picked her up.

"Minna, whatever are you doing, crossing the road — and at this time?" It was after nine-thirty. "Have you come out of school?"

The child shook her head, without speaking.

"You haven't been in to school, yet?"

Again a silent shake of the head.

"Right." Kirsty put her down on the pavement. "Come on, sweetheart. We'll just put my big box in the pick-up, and then we'll go and find Miss Pinder, shall we?"

"I'm hungry, Kirsty. May I have a biscuit, please?"

Kirsty smiled. "Of course, love, but you must eat it quickly. It wouldn't do to be eating in class. You can have a few more for playtime."

Concerned only with the safety of the child on the road, she had not noticed her condition until she removed her coat in the school cloakroom. The blonde hair was unbrushed, the pocket of her dress torn down. The soiled white socks falling about her ankles were not even a pair.

Later — milking and feeding her stock, dusting over the furniture at Tall Trees in readiness for the master's return — Kirsty could not forget the child's forlorn state.

Saturday tomorrow. Perhaps Leif would be home. Yet suppose he wasn't?

Timothy could have coped. He was made of sterner stuff, but Minna was used to being loved and protected.

Remembering the woebegone little face, Kirsty resolved to do something.

★ ★ ★

It was the sun, glaring through the window of the pick-up, softening the vinyl seats, which brought the solution to mind. The woman in the shop would be pleased — the weather was certainly fine, so far.

Of course. Why not take Minna to the garden party? Leila might be pleased to have the child off her hands for a while.

Kirsty was about to pick up the telephone, when it rang.

"Brian Hurst," the voice informed her. "Do you think I could take Timothy home for the weekend? My wife's dying to meet him."

"I should think that would be all right," Kirsty agreed.

His father could hardly wait. "If you would pack a few things for him, I could meet you outside the school and take him from there."

Kirsty smiled. Timothy was assured a

263

good weekend; now for Minna.

Her prayers were answered. To her surprise, Leila seemed willing — even anxious — to see the child depart.

Encouraged, Kirsty offered to collect Minna from school that evening along with Timothy, and was amazed when this, too, was seized upon. If it was Leif's intention to conduct a pre-marital experiment on motherhood, Leila was going to prove a miserable failure.

She packed a suitcase, and set off early for school. The arrangements were going to come as a complete surprise to both children.

Certain of his delight at the prospect of a weekend away, Timothy's reaction was unexpected. "When's Mr. A. coming back, Miss?"

Kirsty shrugged. "This weekend some-time. I'm not sure exactly when. Why do you ask?"

"Will you be all right, Miss, on your own?"

Kirsty could have laughed. Instead, she answered his question with all seriousness. "Yes, love, I'll be fine, thank you. You go ahead and enjoy yourself."

Minna's reaction, on the other hand, was entirely predictable.

A little subdued on hearing that she was being returned to Leila Fennel, she brightened noticeably when Kirsty outlined the plans for the next day, and, leaving her with Mr. Pratley at Leila's gate, Kirsty was happy to see her smiling as she waved goodbye.

★ ★ ★

The weather on Saturday exceeded all hopes. From early morning the sun shone, lifting Kirsty's spirits with its promise of a perfect afternoon.

With her usual morning tasks completed in record time, Kirsty took a trip to Tall Trees to collect fresh clothes for Minna and, at twelve-thirty, unable to contain her eagerness any longer, she got herself ready.

The clock had dominated her morning, but now there was nothing left to do before going to pick up Minna. She could relax; spend the last half-hour or so quietly in the chair with a nice cup of coffee.

She was not to get so far as pouring it out. As she lifted the percolator from the stove, a sudden agonised bleating from the paddock sent her bolting through the door, and across the yard. A glance over the gate, and horror arrested her flight, momentarily rooting her to the spot. Howling at the top of her voice, Mabel struggled franticaly to free her leg, held fast to the blackthorn bushes by a coil of barbed wire.

Where it had come from, Kirsty could not imagine. She had seen none about the place, and would have disposed of it very quickly if she had. Trust Mabel to find it — and find it now, when time was getting short.

The wire cutters were in the barn. Huge, and not as sharp as they might have been, they made little impression when wielded by Kirsty's small hands.

Running back to the house, she snatched up the telephone. The vet. She would have to call him straight away. With shaking hands, she dialled the number, willing him to answer quickly. "Come on, come on. There's got to be someone there. There's got to be . . . "

Clearly there wasn't. Jenny Carter, then. Again she dialled and waited. She was a long time. Feeding her own goats, perhaps? She wouldn't be out, too, would she? Where would she have gone, with Harry away?

Dismayed, she remembered. The garden party. Everyone would be out. She would have been out herself if it had happened a few minutes later. There was no one to help. Somehow she would have to manage.

Throwing a white overall over her dress, she raced back to the paddock. Now blood was oozing down the leg from the torn flesh where Mabel had pulled. If she could just force the loop apart, instead of cutting it, the animal might be able to pull the leg free. Desperately, she tried to untwist the spiky coil, but it was no use. The strand was too thick, and the animal too frightened to keep still.

She went back to the barn to find something else, tipping the old tool-box out on the floor. Surely she must have something to cut it. Pliers — no. Chisel — not that, either. Small hacksaw.

She pounced on it, scrambling to her feet, rushing across the yard, and had almost reached the paddock gate when Leif's Bentley passed the farm gate on its way to Tall Trees.

He was home. Thank heaven he was home. Hacksaw in hand, she rushed back to the house and dialled the number, allowing the ringing to go on and on until he was indoors.

At last the receiver was lifted.

"Leif, it's Kirsty. I know you've just arrived home this minute, and I'm sorry, but could you come? I need help."

"What's the trouble, Kirsty?"

How good it was to hear his voice. Quickly, she explained, trying not to sound as tearful as she felt.

"I'll be there directly." He soon was, striding into the yard, his own wirecutters in his hand.

She ran to meet him. "Thank you for coming." She indicated the paddock. "She's in there."

He smiled. "So I hear."

How skilful the huge hands proved to be. One snip, while Kirsty held her head, and Mabel was free from the bush; two, and the wire could be removed altogether.

In the stable, Leif inspected the wound. "A cleanse with antiseptic solution, and she'll be fine," he assured her. "Healthy goats heal remarkably well."

Within five minutes it was done, and Mabel was resting in her own pen.

"You'll have a cup of coffee, Leif?" Drying her hands, Kirsty turned to him.

He shook his head. "I think not, thank you."

He was about to move away, when Kirsty faced him squarely, looking straight up into his face. "What have I done, Leif — or not done? You used not to refuse to take coffee with me."

From the house, the tinny sound of the telephone filtered. Kirsty clicked her tongue. "There's the phone. Please don't go, Leif. Come to the house. I have to talk to you."

She ran from the stable door to the telephone, arriving breathless.

When the voice came, she could have laughed.

"It's Tim, Miss. Are you all right?"

"Yes, I'm fine, thank you. Are you?"

269

He ignored her question. "Is Mr. A. back yet?"

Kirsty smiled as Leif's tall frame filled the doorway.

"Yes, he's here with me now, as a matter of fact."

"You sure, Miss?"

Kirsty blinked at the receiver. "I'll put him on, if you don't believe me." She turned to Leif. "Would you mind saying hello to Timothy, just to prove you are here?"

Obediently, Leif came forward. "Hello, Timothy."

He handed the receiver back to Kirsty without waiting for an answer.

"Now do you believe me?" she demanded of the boy.

"Yes, Miss. You'll be all right now, then?"

"Yes, thank you, Timothy. I'll be quite all right. You go ahead and enjoy your weekend. See you on Sunday. 'Bye."

Replacing the receiver, she laughed. "He seems to consider himself my lord and protector while you're away."

The truth — but what a stupid thing

to say. Feeling her face flush, she turned away quickly, reaching for the mugs and placing them on the table.

"Where is the boy?"

"Spending the weekend with . . . " Kirsty hesitated, and her features broke into a wide smile. "Shall I tell you a secret?"

"I think I have guessed it already." His eyes met hers steadily.

★ ★ ★

Kirsty gave a delighted laugh. "You have? I hoped you would. Isn't it marvellous — the best thing that could ever happen?" Her eyes sparkled.

He remained unsmiling. "I suppose it is, for you."

"For me?" She blinked. "Well, not particularly for me — but for Timothy. He's the important one, isn't he?"

"And you are not?"

Kirsty shrugged. "Not in this case, no."

"You think you are going to be happy?" Far from pleased, he sounded exasperated. She was unable to follow

271

his line of thought.

"It makes no difference to me, does it?"

"Of course, it does!" Without warning, Leif leapt to his feet, shaking the table, making the mugs rattle. "It makes all the difference. Clearly, you are not . . . in love . . . with this man, and . . . "

"In love?" Kirsty's mouth fell open, and she almost dropped the sugar basin. "In love? What on earth are you talking about? I think the world would come to an end before I was in love with Timothy's father — nice man, though he is."

Leif stared at her. "He is the boy's father?"

She nodded. "Brian Hurst. Timothy's natural father. We didn't think he had one. That is to say, we thought he had disappeared into the blue long ago. It seems now that he didn't leave the mother — it was the other way round. He didn't know of any forthcoming child at the time."

He nodded. "I see. So he had no idea of the existence of the boy?"

"None at all," she explained. "He

asked me to introduce him as 'Uncle Brian', so that Timothy didn't suspect the truth, and, as far as I know, he still doesn't. The idea is that he doesn't feel under any pressure, while they get to know each other."

She laughed suddenly. "I felt under pressure that first evening. I wished you had stayed, Leif. I didn't know the man at all. It was most difficult trying to make conversation."

He regarded her thoughtfully. "You have always been able to talk to me."

She shrugged. "You're different."

"How?"

"Well, you're a lot taller, and your hair's a different colour, and you're Norwegian, and . . . " Kirsty laughed as he drew his eyebrows together in a frown. "Oh, I don't know. You just are, that's all. Anyway, the important thing is that Timothy gets on with him like a house on fire. I really couldn't see a happy end for him, and this is like a dream come true. A fairytale." She beamed up at him. "I'm so excited about it, I could dance, or sing, or . . . "

"Do something equally silly," He

moved closer. "Something like this, perhaps?"

Before she could grasp his intention, his strong arms plucked her from the chair, holding her close while his lips sought hers in a tender, unhurried kiss.

Too soon he set her back on her feet, yet still his smiling eyes sought hers. "You are happy that I am back, Kirsty?"

"Oh, yes," she breathed, causing him to give a shaky little laugh.

"I, too, am happy." Moving back to his chair, his eye caught the pile of clothes at the other end of the table.

"Minna's," she confirmed. "I'm picking her up at one-thirty to take her to the garden party."

Leif consulted his watch. "It's after that time now."

Balancing precariously on one leg, she began dragging at one of her green wellingtons. "I'm late. She'll think I'm not coming."

"Sit down, Kirsty." He was laughing. "It's no great tragedy if you're a few minutes late." Dropping on one knee, he calmly pulled off her boot.

"You don't know that," Kirsty wailed. "Suppose they leave her? What would have happened yesterday morning, if I hadn't happened to be there?"

He regarded her seriously, blue eyes raking her anxious face. "I don't know, Kirsty. Perhaps you had better tell me."

"I don't know, either." Kirsty muttered the words, and looked away.

"Kirsty." He waited until she looked back at him. "I shall find out — and I would rather hear it from someone I know to be truthful."

"All right," she sighed, "if I must."

Quickly, she gave him a run-down on the events of the week, ending with the last time she had seen Minna. "It was the only time I left her smiling, and now I've let her down."

"Come on." He stood up, holding out his hand. "We go for her together."

Sitting beside him, Minna's clothes on her knee, it seemed almost as if they were a family. Remembering his kiss, his strong hand holding hers as they crossed the yard, she felt warm and protected — as if nothing could ever hurt her again.

Although Kirsty had passed the entrance to Fennel Farm Associates on countless occasions, she had never been to the house.

"I should like you to go for her, Kirsty," Leif requested, as he switched off the engine.

Kirsty blinked. "Why? Minna will be so thrilled to see you."

He smiled. "Ja, but I am not thinking of Minna. I should like to observe Leila."

She shrugged. "Well, if you insist."

The large door knocker appeared to be brass, but was unexpectedly light and made a hollow tinny sound. Kirsty waited a while, then tried it again. Leif remained round the corner, outside the porch.

"Oh, there you are at last." Coming to the door, after Kirsty's third attempt, Leila said, "Took your time, didn't you?"

"I had a problem with one of the goats," Kirsty explained cheerfully. "Sorry I'm late. Is Minna ready?"

Leila shrugged. "I expect so. The last time I saw her, she was outside the door, whining because you hadn't come."

276

"When was that?" Kirsty struggled to keep calm. "How long ago?"

"I haven't the faintest idea." Already the door was closing. "If you want to find her, I suggest you go and look."

The door slammed, and Kirsty found herself trembling with the struggle to control her rising temper. There was no need to say anything to Leif. His expression made it clear that he had heard every word.

"Minna! Minna!" They shouted in unison. There was no reply.

"Minna!" As they tried for the second time, the house door was flung wide, and Leila came forward into the porch.

"Leif, how lovely. You're home. We're so worried. Miss Trensham seems to have lost little Minna."

Leif frowned. "Miss Trensham and I travelled together, in my car. I understood, from your exchange, that Minna was missing before we arrived."

Leila flushed, and said nothing more.

"Shall I go that way, and you go the other?" Kirsty indicated with her hand. "She can't be far away, surely. I'm not all that late."

277

Kirsty checked a log store, and high barn, before coming to another, windowless building, partially demolished. One wall was in a state of collapse, a gaping hole in the roof, it seemed a most unlikely place, but Kirsty decided that she must check all the same.

The lower hinge had dropped on the left side, causing the heavy wooden door to scrape across the floor, shaking the whole building as she moved cautiously forward, peering into the depths.

"Minna! Are you there, darling?"

She was about to move back outside, when a small whimper came from somewhere ahead. In that same moment, as her eyes became more accustomed to the ill-lit interior, she saw, to her horror, that the floor in the corner had fallen in.

"Minna!" Her call was louder now, more anxious. "Minna! Where are you, darling?"

The mumbled reply left her in no doubt. Minna was down the hole.

"Leif!" Her shriek brought him running, with Leila following. "The whole place is falling down. What can we do? Oh God, what can we do?"

"Steady, Kirsty." His hand came on her shoulder, gently giving strength. "Let us consider our moves carefully."

Calmer now that he was beside her, Kirsty's eyes travelled round the interior of the building. After a moment, she pointed upward to the roof, above the hole in the floor.

"Would that beam support my weight on a rope, do you think?"

Leif stared at her. "You are not going to try. I shall go." He stopped as she took hold of his arm, restraining him.

"You'd never get down there, Leif. Look at the size of the hole. You would have the whole building down on top of her, if you try." It was true, and she could see by his expression that he knew it.

"I'll go down. I can climb a rope — and no doubt get down without touching the sides too much." She waited for his answer, but when none came, she grasped his arm. "Leif, it's our only chance. For pity's sake, let's do something — Minna's down there!"

He gave a quick nod, and took charge.

"Ladder, Leila, and a rope. Where are they kept?"

She indicated the large barn, and he sprinted towards it, returning a few moments later with a coil of rope over his shoulder, and a ladder in one hand.

For a moment after he placed it in position, his eyes held Kirsty's. "I must risk going up myself. You could not fasten the rope. Go outside, Kirsty, just in case . . ."

He left the rest unsaid, as Kirsty moved back and watched him inch his tall frame up the ladder, to fix the rope on the beam and drop it carefully to dangle into the hole.

"Kirsty, are you sure?" Back on the ground, his eyes raked her face. "I pulled on the beam. It's solid at the moment, but . . . ?"

There was no need to climb the ladder to its full length. Halfway up, she could reach the rope, and was about to transfer when a thought came. How was she going to get the child out? Could Minna cling to her back throughout the arduous climb? Suppose she lost her grip part-way?

"Do you have a long strap?" she called. "Something I could use to . . . "

There was no need to explain. Looking down, she found Leif holding up his leather belt. "You will need this."

Seconds later, the belt fastened round her, bandolier style, Kirsty was on the rope, poised above the hole.

"Minna!" she called.

"Kirsty." The answer was a sobbing cry.

"That's right, darling. Now listen to me. I'm coming down to get you, but I'm a lot bigger than you are, so I won't slide down so easily. I may knock bits down on to you, so I want you to do something for me. All right?"

"Please come, Kirsty."

"I'm coming, love," Kirsty said gently, "but first you must do this for me. Now shut your eyes really tight, and clasp your hands behind your neck. Will you do that for me, Minna?"

Minna whimpered. "It's all muddy."

"Never mind the mud, darling. You can have a nice shower when you get home. Now have you done that — eyes shut, and hands clasped?"

"Yes."

"Good girl," Kirsty said warmly.

Swiftly she made the descent. It was farther down than she expected. A well, judging by the feel of the damp air. Would the rope be long enough to reach the bottom? It was. Suddenly her toes were touching thick, oozing mud. She was there — but where was the child?

"It's dark, Kirsty." In the depths, the sobbing voice echoed.

Kirsty reached out. "Never mind, love. We'll have to be little candles, won't we? Do you remember the song I taught you about a little candle?"

★ ★ ★

Miraculously, the child seemed not to be hurt, only shocked and frightened. All the time that she knelt in the mud, persuading the little girl to cling to her neck, using Leif's belt to strap the small body against her back, Kirsty kept up a ceaseless chatter to keep the child's mind — and her own — away from their dark, damp surroundings.

Struggling upward, with the child's

added weight — her ribs still bruised from the assault by Timothy's stepfather — it was not as easy as she envisaged.

As they neared the top of the hole, the air became sweeter. Her hands and arms were out of the hole. Now her head, now Minna's head. Waiting a moment, gasping for breath, she caught a quick movement from the doorway and turned her head to see Leif, about to approach.

"No!" She gave a few hurried breaths, struggling to get out what she wanted to say. "It's not safe — any of it — all open underneath."

In spite of her warning, they were still only just clear of the ground when he leapt forward, plucking them off the rope, crushing them both into his arms and burying his face in their hair.

"Leif, your clothes!" Crouching down, while he unbuckled his belt and let Minna free, she surveyed them in horror. The expensive, well-cut slacks, and cream hand-made shirt, were daubed with greenish black slime.

"Does it matter? Let's get you home."

At the gate of Refuge, seeing him

about to pass, she had to remind him that this was her home.

"You have no hot water, Kirsty. You must come to Tall Trees," he insisted.

"I shall need some clean clothes, then," she laughed, "if you wouldn't mind fetching them. They wouldn't be clean any longer, if I did."

She was not laughing a short time later, under the shower. Reasonably calm and capable at the time, she now began to shake violently and, struggling to dry the little girl, she had to clench her teeth hard to stop them openly chattering.

"Can I stay and wait for you?" Perched on the stool, in her dressing-gown, Minna's face was wreathed in smiles.

Unable to speak, Kirsty nodded. Stupid to feel like this, now the danger was past.

Holding her head down for the last rinse, she felt decidedly giddy. Quickly, she gripped the knob and turned off the shower.

As she carefully straightened up, reaching to swish back the shower curtain, an excruciating pain shot through her side. Her face drained. With a sharp cry of agony, she clutched at her ribs, fighting to overcome the nausea, as a cold sweat began to pour down her face.

"Oh, Minna," she breathed, closing her eyes and then opening them again. "Minna, I feel so . . . "

"Kirsty!" Vaguely, she saw the little girl scrambling from the stool.

The child's anxious cry was the last thing Kirsty heard.

"Ah! At last."

Kirsty's eyes flickered.

"What happened?" She put a limp hand to her head, and a loose sleeve brushed her face. "What am I wearing?"

Leif smiled. "It's my shirt. I was about to put it on when I heard Minna shout to me."

"Oh yes." Her eyes dropped shut, then opened again. "The shower. I remember. Thank you."

He grinned. "Vaer sa god."

She blinked up at him, still rather dazed. "What does than mean, exactly?"

Leif pursed his lips. "You are welcome . . . It's my pleasure." He smiled. "In this case, my great pleasure."

Kirsty blushed. "I'm sorry about all this. So stupid."

He smiled. "It's simply delayed shock, I think. However, the doctor has been summoned, just to be on the safe side."

Ten minutes later, in Minna's bedroom, Dr. Taylor felt round her ribs carefully, his eyes fixed on her face.

"Yes," he pronounced, "we'll strap you up again, and this time I want no gymnastics, young lady. No exertion, no lifting whatsoever. All right?"

Kirsty nodded.

"Very good." Taking up his stethoscope, he turned to Minna.

"Now what about you, young Miss Fennel?"

Miss Fennel? Carefully sitting up, Kirsty smiled. Dr. Taylor was getting mixed up. She was called Minna Amundsen. Clearly, the name must have been changed at some time, since Leif had never married — previously her name would have been that of the mother. Anyway, Leila was the only one of her family left, so Minna's name could never have been Fennel — that is, unless . . . ? It was a mistake, wasn't it? It had to be.

Slowly she dressed, while the doctor made his examination of the child.

"She seems to be fine." He smiled, at last. "Keep her quiet for the rest of the day, and you should have no trouble. I'll give her a mild sedative just in case she should need it tonight, but I very much doubt it."

He drew out his prescription pad from his bag.

"Let's see, what is it?" He smiled at Minna. "Miss M.B. Fennel, if I remember rightly, from when I brought you into the world."

Numb with shock, Kirsty stood up, her eyes fixed on the little girl's laughing face as she agreed with the doctor.

It was true — no slip of the tongue — and suddenly everything clicked into place. This was the reason that Leila had gone to Norway, the reason that Minna had been left in her care. She had taken it to be a pre-marital experiment. Instead, the bond was much stronger.

Leif had called her a spiteful, jealous woman, and so she was — but not without cause. She was fighting desperately to keep her man. This should be her place, here in Leif's house, the mistress of Tall Trees. She had borne his child. Leila Fennel was Minna's mother.

Kirsty gathered together her muddy clothes. "I've got to go and feed the goats now, Minna. Farbror Leif will be back in a moment. I'll see you another day."

Downstairs in the kitchen, Leif was pouring coffee.

"Oh, Leif. Could you run me home, please? I have to see to the goats." She struggled to make her voice sound natural, and failed.

He straightened, putting down the pot. "It's too early for the goats and you intended to spend the afternoon with Minna. I thought we could all . . ."

"No." Kirsty shook her head. "I'll go home, if you don't mind, Leif."

He remained perfectly still, regarding her steadily. "I do mind. I mind very much. I had gained the impression that you felt the same as me." He hesitated, his eyes raking her face. "Something has happened to upset you?"

She made no answer.

"It's because I kissed you?"

"No!" Her fervent denial was out

before she could stop it.

"Because upstairs just now I had to . . . ?"

She shook her head, miserably.

"Then if it is not me, it must be the child. I thought you loved Minna."

"I do." Tears came into Kirsty's eyes. "You know I do."

He spread his hands. "Then I cannot understand you, Kirsty."

"It's not because . . ." Kirsty fought for control. "It's who she is. If she were my child — but she isn't, Leif. She never would be."

"But she is mine, Kirsty." His voice was quiet now, resigned. "I cannot give her up."

"I wouldn't want you to." Desperately, Kirsty tried to make him see the position from her point of view. "The fact that she is yours makes it totally different for you. Don't you see that, for me, it would be an impossible situation?"

To be between a man and the woman who had borne his child. To love and cherish her, only to have her real mother demand to have charge of her whenever the fancy took her?

She became aware that Leif was speaking. "Pardon . . . ?"

"I asked if you thought you could ever come to terms with the situation?"

Not when Leila was so near. Just up the road. And how could she ask him to move away — leave his lovely home, and his business?

Sadly, she gazed at him. "I'm sorry."

He sighed. "Then there's nothing more to be said. I cannot pretend that I am not disappointed. You seemed to be so happy that I am home and . . . "

"Don't, Leif, please." At any moment she would burst into tears. "I'll continue to help you, of course. Come in to work as usual, and . . . "

He straightened, hooking his thumbs in his belt. "I think not, Kirsty. It's best to make a clean break — ja? Minna and I can manage."

Kirsty made no answer and, leaving the coffee, he moved to the door. "You are ready?"

She had to be. This was another woman's place, not hers. She must go. Go now. Leave everything that she had come to hold dear. And not look back — lest she run into his arms.

The moment he left her at Refuge, Kirsty broke down completely, sobbing uncontrollably for a life that was not to be. In the space of one afternoon, she had won and lost the only man she would ever love. Yet the fact that she did love him, with every fibre of her being, made no difference. How could she, knowingly, separate the child's parents?

7

IT was some hours before she noticed the piece of paper on the floor, just inside the door. Folded neatly, it was clearly a note, and automatically she moved across to pick it up.

To her surprise, it was from Brian Hurst. A request to keep Timothy for the spring bank holiday.

Kirsty stared at the paper in her hand. Spring bank holiday? Timothy hadn't mentioned it, nor had anyone else. Normally she would have checked with Leif, asked about Minna; now she dared not make contact.

She rang Miss Pinder — a brief, pointed call, which was to be her last contact with the outside world for more than a week. The house neglected, Kirsty roamed the woods. Alone and tormented, her long hair windswept, her mind registering nothing of the wild iris and blue water forget-me-not at the edge of the river, nor the song of the larks overhead — it did not occur to her that she would be missed. Only the goats received her regular attention.

When, on the Monday, nine days after she had parted from Leif, she arrived home in the middle of the day to find Jenny sitting in her pick-up, she could only stare silently in surprise. Jenny was somewhat more eloquent.

"Right!" She pushed the pick-up door shut with the walking stick, to which she had graduated. "What's the trouble?"

"I'm all right." Hunched into her duffle coat, hands in pockets, Kirsty failed to meet her eyes.

"I've got eyes and ears, young woman. You don't look all right, and you don't sound all right. You don't go to the village. You don't answer your telephone. Not like you. Not like you, at all."

Along the road, a large van, followed by two or three cars, drowned the sound of Jenny's voice. She watched them pass.

"Not more reporters ringing his door-bell, I hope. He's already like a bear with a sore head, Harry says. Wouldn't have anything to do with you, I suppose?"

Kirsty shrugged without speaking.

Jenny's eyes flicked over her, then she moved round, opened the house door, and inclined her head sharply towards it. Obediently, Kirsty stepped inside, to stand motionless in the middle of the floor while Jenny filled the kettle, and brought two cups to the table. She was talking all the time.

"Something to do with this press story, is it?"

"Press story?" Kirsty blinked.

"Where've you been, young woman? The whole place is buzzing with it."

Kirsty pulled out a chair and sat down, dropping her head on to her arms. "I haven't heard."

"Time you did then." Jenny banged a steaming cup in front of her, spun a chair, and plonked down astride it, her elbows resting on the back. "Now just sit up and listen. Young Leif Amundsen is the hero of the day, right now. Seems his grandfather was that pleased with the way he took on to look after the bairn, that he's remembered him in his will. That's what this last trip to Norway was all about."

"I see." Still sounding bleak, Kirsty

294

nevertheless took a sip of coffee. "The newspapers are covering the story, then?"

"That's it, young woman. A bit of well-deserved praise, I say."

"I suppose so."

"Do you? To me it sounds as if you don't think he's making a good enough job of it."

Kirsty looked up hastily into Jenny's accusing eyes.

"Oh no, it's not that," she tried to explain. "He's making a marvellous job of bringing up Minna. It's just that ... well ... he's not the only single parent around, and I wonder if the grandfather would have done the same thing for Minna's mother, if she'd taken on the child alone."

Jenny frowned. "Say again, young woman?"

Kirsty sighed. "It doesn't matter. I know Leif is good with Minna and Leila is awful — and that it's unusual for a father to have custody of a girl that age. It just seems to be remarkable good fortune to have such recognition for bringing up your own child."

"What the heck are you blathering

about?" Jenny made no bones about her feelings. "Minna is Brunhilde's child, not Leif's."

"Brunhilde?" Hazel eyes stared wide from the deathly pale face. "Who is Brunhilde?"

Jenny looked shocked. "Leif's twin sister, of course. Has no one ever told you?"

★ ★ ★

Into Kirsty's mind came a picture of the silver-framed photograph in Leif's office. She shook her head.

"Then," Jenny exploded, "it's about time somebody did."

And Kirsty found herself listening, with growing horror, to the sad story.

Brunhilde's husband, Robin — Leila's brother — was Leif's college friend, and the new manager of Tall Trees. He was bringing his wife out of hospital, after Minna was born, when a truck hit the car. Brunhilde had been killed outright; Robin completely paralysed. The baby escaped unhurt.

Leif had been staying with the couple

to help them get settled in their new home, and he had simply taken over. Refusing to believe that Robin would not improve in time, he had soldiered on — managing the farm and bringing up the child. On Robin's death, he became legally what in reality he had always been — Minna's guardian and only father.

As Jenny finished her tale, Kirsty stared at her in silence. What torment Leif must have suffered. His twin sister killed, his best friend totally paralysed, he had struggled for five years to bring up their child. And when he had been on the point of asking her to stand by him in his ordeal, she had backed away.

She stood up. "I must go to him, Jenny. If only someone had told me before I made such a terrible mistake."

"I should go and tidy yourself up a bit, before you rush off." Jenny smiled kindly. "Then you can stay awhile. I'll manage everything here."

What a good friend she was, to be sure. Bathing her face, brushing her tangled hair, slipping into a dress, and finally making her way up to Tall Trees, Kirsty was confident that she had left Refuge in safe hands.

When she returned it would be with renewed vigour. For the past nine days, there had seemed no point to anything in her life. The hopes and plans of the previous months had been set aside, while she allowed herself to sink in despair. Now, with her love by her side, anything was possible.

There was no sign of life when she arrived at Tall Trees. Knocking lightly on the door, she entered quietly. It was lunchtime. No doubt someone would be in the kitchen.

She was almost at the door when Leif appeared at the head of the stairs. Kirsty skipped up the bottom step, her eyes shining.

"Oh, there you are, Leif. Excuse me just walking in. I have to see you. I've made such a stupid mistake."

Slowly, silently, he descended the staircase, his eyes cold. "Yes, you made a mistake. And now you have made another."

Stepping round her, he moved down

the last step, crossed the hall, and went into the office.

She followed slowly, stopping a yard inside the room. "Leif?"

He sat down at the desk, tipping his chair back, regarding her.

"Nine days ago you leave me. It's an 'impossible situation'. Now you are back." He made a wry face. "They tell me to expect a queue of young ladies competing for my favours. I did not expect you to be the first."

Kirsty blinked, uncomprehending. "Queue? First? I don't understand."

He threw his weight forward, setting his chair back on its feet with a bang. "You do not understand? You are trying to tell me that your sudden change of heart has nothing to do with this?"

Snatching up a paper with one hand, he hit it so violently with the back of the other that it tore out of his fingers, and flapped to the floor.

He retrieved it, holding it between both hands, turning it to face her. It was part of a newspaper.

"Jenny did say something about it," she confessed, "but she wasn't explicit — and, anyway, it has nothing to do with . . . "

She stopped. Her eyes had flicked from his stony face, back to the newspaper. Suddenly the headline — the glaring large-lettered words — swam off the page, making sense of what he was saying, and striking horror in her heart.

'MILLIONAIRE LEAVES FORTUNE TO GRANDSON'

Millionaire? Fortune? Then he thought . . .

Shaking her head, she backed away.

"I'm sorry, I didn't realise. Jenny didn't say, you see . . . " She swallowed hard, then went on talking to cover her sudden urge to burst into tears . . . "I expect she thought you would know, thought you would trust me . . . as I did."

Suddenly tears were blinding her eyes. Biting her lip, she turned away, clutching at the edge of the door to establish her whereabouts.

"I'm sorry to have taken up so much of your precious time. Goodbye, Leif."

"Wait, Kirsty!" His sharp exclamation arrested her flight. "If that was not your reason for coming, there must be another. I should like to hear it."

She shook her head, sniffing. "It doesn't matter now."

Leif leapt to his feet, sending his chair crashing to the floor.

"And I say it does!"

"All right." She raised her head defiantly. "I'll tell you. I came because Jenny has just told me that Minna is your sister Brunhilde's child."

He leaned heavily on the desk. "Ja, and . . . ?"

"And nothing." Still tearful, she glared at him. "That's it. The whole thing. Why I came."

He straightened, hooking his thumbs in his belt. "You are not making sense, Kirsty. You have said nothing except that Minna is the child of my dear twin sister. This was surely the fact that you found impossible to endure — the reason you would not stay with me, could not think of her as your own?"

"No, it wasn't!" The denial came out as an anguished cry. "I didn't even know you had a twin sister. I've always thought that Minna was your child — your own daughter."

For a moment he stared at her in silence, lips parted and eyes widened in shocked disbelief.

"But you knew that I had never been married."

"Oh come on, Leif. You don't have to be married to have a child. I knew that if you were concerned, it wouldn't be a dishonourable situation, and that was enough for me. I was prepared to accept Minna — until Dr. Taylor called her 'Miss Fennel'. Then, from my point of view, there could be only one explanation. She was not only your child — she was also Leila's.

"That was the situation I said was impossible, and so it would have been. To come between a child's natural parents is a difficult enough position if they are divorced, but when they are as yet unmarried — and the woman so clearly willing — it is unthinkable." She stopped to brush tears from her cheeks with the tips of her fingers. "I never seem to have a handkerchief when I need it most."

Throughout her long revelation Leif

had remained motionless. Now he sprang forward, snatching a white linen handkerchief from his pocket, holding it out. "Here, Kirsty."

How she would have loved to take it; feel its warmth and the momentary touch of his fingers. Instead, she backed away, shaking her head, holding up her hand, palm outwards, to stop him.

"No, I don't want anything from you. That's not why I came, and I wouldn't like my motives to be misconstrued. I hope you find someone to make you happy among your queue of young ladies, Leif."

For a moment, hurt tear-filled eyes centred on his, then she turned sharply and left the room.

As she reached the front door, a voice called from the stairs.

"Kirsty! Kirsty! You're back." The child's face was wreathed in smiles as, arms outstretched, she ran towards her.

Kirsty caught the warm little body, holding her close as she buried her face in the blonde curls. Then Leif stepped out of the office.

Brushing her lips on the smooth cheek,

Kirsty set the child back on her feet. "'Bye, Minna. See you another day." Then, without looking up, she turned and fled the house.

At Refuge, she found Jenny in the kitchen.

"You've still got a face like a wet weekend. What's wrong?"

Kirsty sighed. "Apparently, Leif has been told to expect a queue of young ladies after his money. He supposed that I was the first."

She reached for the tea-towel, methodically drying and putting away the pots that Jenny had washed, talking all the time in an inane, dispassionate way to mask her inner turmoil.

It was to be the pattern of the next few weeks. Dry-eyed now, her behaviour was exactly the opposite to that during the nine days that she had walked the woods. Then she had forgotten the farm — neglected it. Now it became the epitome of efficiency — every chore dealt with in the most meticulous fashion.

So the holidays passed, and Timothy returned to the fold.

"My Dad's being made redundant. He

says he's going to look round for a place like this."

Kirsty looked up from opening the morning mail. So it was 'Dad' now, was it? Clearly Timothy had accepted the news happily.

"What is his job, Timothy?" She slit another envelope. Bills, bills, and more bills.

"He's a saw doctor, Miss. He sharpens the teeth, and stuff. He reckons he could do a lot with a place like this."

No doubt he could. No doubt, if he lived here and worked at his trade, he would make a much better job of it than she had.

"He says if he could rent this place, and work for Mr. A., it'd be a nice little living."

The last letter poised for opening, Kirsty raised her eyebrows.

"Got it all sewn up, have you? And where am I supposed to live, while all this is going on?"

"That's what I said, Miss, but me Dad said you was probably gonna marry Mr. A."

"Well, I'm sorry to disappoint you, but

I'm not. Now off you go and feed the guinea pigs while I finish reading my letters."

She was anxious to examine her last communication more closely — unable to believe the coincidence.

The letter in her hand was none other than an offer of re-instatement at her old position. Since Miss Marshall (Sarah) was about to be married, a vacancy would occur, and as she knew most of the children, they would be pleased to know if she was interested.

Was she? Could she bring herself to leave this lovely place — go back to the city, and never again come face-to-face with the man she loved, or Minna?

Had she a choice? Wasn't it a fact that rising costs would shortly force her out, anyway?

* * *

Just over a week later, outside school, Leif's Range Rover pulled up behind the pick-up. By the gate, Kirsty waited. Would he remain seated, or come to stand beside her?

He got out, straightening to the incredible height which constantly surprised her, and approached without hesitation. "You are well, Kirsty?"

"Yes, thank you — and you?"

"Fine."

Polite conversation, between semi-strangers. He didn't look well. He looked gaunt and tired. Too many late nights, perhaps?

He consulted his watch. "Three-thirty exactly. They will soon . . . "

Even as he spoke, the door opened and dozens of children spilled forth, their excited voices preventing any further exchange.

As she watched for her particular charge, from out of a small knot of children by the door, came Minna.

"Kirsty! Kirsty!" Arms outstretched, running as fast as her little legs would go, she skirted Leif to fling herself into Kirsty's arms.

"Hey, what's all this?" Kirsty gave her a quick hug, then set her on her feet. To her surprise, she found the little girl tearful, and accusing.

"Timothy says you're going away, and

his family is going to live in your house."

Kirsty smoothed back a strand of blonde hair. "It's possible, Minna."

"I don't want you to go."

Kirsty gave a warm smile. "I don't want to, either, Minna, but sometimes circumstances force us to do things that we don't particularly like."

The little girl ran a finger down Kirsty's face.

"I'm frightened of his family."

"Frightened?" Kirsty threw a puzzled glance at Leif. "Why, darling?"

"He says his family tells him things."

"What sort of things, Minna?"

The child pressed closer. "Things about me."

Kirsty frowned. "But they don't know you. His daddy is the only one who has been here, and he hardly saw you."

"It's not his daddy. It's that toad."

"The toad?" Kirsty's eyes widened. Then, suddenly, light dawned. "Wait a minute. He didn't say 'family', did he, Minna? A word very like it, but not quite. 'Familiar'." She pronounced the word very carefully. "'Familiar' — that was the word, wasn't it?"

"Yes." The child's face puckered.

"He's been saying that he knows things that are going to happen to you?"

"Yes."

Kirsty took the child gently by the shoulders and held her away, looking deep into her eyes.

"Now listen to me, Minna. It just isn't true. Nobody — nobody at all — can tell even the smallest thing that is going to happen. It's a trick, and it only works because Timothy has made you believe he can do it."

"But . . . " Minna sniffed. " . . . he knows other things about me."

Kirsty nodded. "Yes. That's how it's done. He has asked questions — found out things that you thought he wouldn't know — and told you he got the information from the toad."

Round blue eyes stared unblinking into her own, trusting, yet still unable to accept that there was nothing to fear.

"Look, Minna." Kirsty came to a decision. "I'll give you a practical demonstration. You know that the first time Farbror Leif and I met was in March, just a few months ago?"

The little girl nodded, and Kirsty smiled.

"Right. I'm going to tell him something that happened years ago, when he was about twenty-one years old."

Gently, Kirsty turned the child round to face Leif.

"Now look at his face. Already he is puzzled, and that's the way the trick works. Like this."

Covering her eyes with her hand, she was silent for a moment. Then she said, "I'm getting a picture. It's a bit hazy . . . coming clearer. Ah, now I see."

Slowly, as if the scene was actually before her at that moment, she described exactly what Leif had been wearing on the day, all those years ago, when she accidently turned the hose-pipe on him.

"Grey trousers — blue grey, with a fleck, like tweed. Leather belt — not as wide as the one you wear now, and with a buckle like a shield, or crest, headed by a crown. Blue shirt with a stripe — not a coloured stripe, but a blue silky thread in the material. Open-necked style."

She gave a little laugh. "You didn't have a beard then. Thinner, too, more boyish frame . . . That's all I can see. No wait. Cuff-links. Very unusual cuff-links." She took her hand away, and opened her eyes. "Well, how did I do?"

A glance at Leif told her and, looking from one astonished face to the other, she laughed.

"Actually, you see, it's all nonsense. I only know what Farbror Leif was wearing that day because I was there."

Leif frowned. "You were there?"

She nodded. "That's right. I was the awful child who turned the hose-pipe on you." She threw him a rueful glance before bending down again to the child's level. "So you see, Minna, it's all a trick, and there's no need to be afraid."

Minna curled her arms round Kirsty's neck. "I don't want you to go."

Kirsty smiled. "Well, it won't be for a little while yet, and I'm sure you'll find Mr. and Mrs. Hurst very nice neighbours."

By the school door, the knot of children began to disperse, and she saw Timothy coming forward.

"Ah!" Kirsty stood up, "Mr. Merlin — who will be familiar with the sleight

311

of my hand before he's very much older."
She ran her fingers lightly over Minna's
bright curls. "'Bye, Minna. See you
another day."

"'Bye, Leif." She gave him the briefest
glance, before moving off across the
playground — deliberately casual, as if
it mattered little whether or not she saw
him again.

She tackled Timothy back at Refuge.
"Now then, young man. It seems you've
been frightening Minna with talk of
Turnip being your 'familiar'?"

"That's right, Miss." He was unashamed.

"But why, Timothy? What has she ever
done to you?"

"Nothin', Miss." For a moment he
stood, silently sullen, then he blurted out,
"But he's treated you rotten, Miss."

Kirsty stared, aghast. "You haven't
tried to frighten Minna in a misguided
attempt at revenge, have you?"

The boy stood silent.

Kirsty sighed. "Oh, Timothy! I'm sure
you meant to protect me, and for that
I'm grateful, but that little girl could
dream about this for weeks. Now the
moment you get to school tomorrow, I

want you to seek out Minna and tell her that it wasn't true, and that you're very, very, sorry. Promise me, now."

"Promise, Miss." Eyes downcast, he stood scuffing the toe of one shoe on the floor.

"Look, Tim . . . " Kirsty put a hand on his shoulder . . . "From Mr. Amundsen's point of view — and it is quite understandable — I didn't want to be friends until he was rich." She sighed. "I thought he knew me better, that's all."

"So did I, Miss." Looking down into the face brimming with defiant loyalty, Kirsty capitulated altogether. How could she be angry when his only thought had been to make amends for her own raw deal. Instead, she smiled.

"You won't lose out, Tim. I've almost decided to go back to my old job, which will leave this place empty for you, if your father would like to rent it. I've already spoken to him about it and, if he decides to go ahead, you'll still be Mr. Amundsen's nearest neighbours — so just you make sure of giving that apology. I shall ask you about it first

313

thing tomorrow evening."

She did. The next evening, and the next — and the next. The days passed — a week, ten days — and still the answer was the same.

"She's not at school, Miss. Miss Pinder says she's poorly."

"First thing on Monday, then," was her parting shot as, with a grin and a wave, he climbed into his father's car for yet another weekend away.

Kirsty stared after the receding vehicle, her smile fading.

Minna had been ill a long time. Could it have been sparked off by Timothy's indiscretion? How awful it was to have no news at all of the two people about whom she cared most. Leif must be at his wits' end. Would he ring her if he needed help?

"Don't be stupid, Kirsty Trensham." Shutting the gate with a snap, she took herself inside. "You're not the only pebble on the beach — he made that very clear. If he does need help, there'll be plenty of other sources he can tap. On Monday, no doubt, both children will be back at school and the crisis over."

314

Her thoughts, at that moment, would have been a good example to Minna of how unpredictable the future can be. On Sunday, Brian Hurst telephoned.

"The lad's under the weather — our doctor says it's tonsillitis. He might as well stay here until he's better, don't you think?"

Kirsty agreed with a heavy heart. Better for the boy, it certainly was; that things had worked out well for Timothy was the one bright spot.

At five-fifteen on Monday afternoon she was by the gate. "Any news of Minna, Harry?"

He stopped his bicycle, and came over. "'Fraid not, lass. Haven' seen anyone today. Doctor stayed a fair old while, and the only time I saw young Leif was when he was leaving. Neither looked too happy, I can tell you that. Why don't you go up, see if there's anything you can do? I'm sure he'd appreciate it, lass."

Kirsty shook her head. "I'm sure he wouldn't, Harry. He made his thoughts about me very plain the last time I was up there."

As the week dragged on, Kirsty kept

herself occupied every moment of the daylight hours, afraid that if she allowed herself a moment's respite, the worry and heartache would cause her to break down completely.

On Thursday morning, a silver-lettered envelope arrived in the post. Edged with hearts and flowers, the card inside announced that she was 'cordially invited to the marriage of Sarah and Monty'. So it had got to that stage?

Her eye flicked over the standard wording to the date. Saturday, the — what? She sat up, eyes flicking from the card to the calendar, and back again. It was this Saturday — two days away!

A small sheet of paper explained: 'Dear Kirsty,' it read. 'Sorry about the short notice, but I didn't want you spending your hard-earned pennies on a present. After all, what can you buy for someone who has everything, and that's just what I intend to have from now on . . . '

The words blurred. Even this was not good news. The message, so mercenary, and unlike the Sarah she knew, was the last straw. Kirsty dissolved into tears.

★ ★ ★

The wedding of Sarah and Monty was exactly as Kirsty had feared, and — presumably — the bride hoped. Mountains of food weighed down damask-covered tables in the flower-decked marquee; champagne overflowed; the cake — bedecked in silver leaves, horseshoes, and ribbon — numbered a massive five tiers.

The bride, resplendent in satin, stitched with tiny pearls, presided over the hundred-strong guests with an attitude more of satisfaction than enthusiasm.

Unable to talk to her friend in the way she would have liked, Kirsty stood in a corner, a fixed smile on her face. She stayed only as long as absolutely necessary, and cried all the way home.

Exhausted, she fell into bed after midnight, only to toss about restlessly as she attempted to push all worrying thoughts from her mind. When, at last, she did sleep it was a troubled rest, full of fears and shadows.

She woke suddenly, raising herself on one elbow to peer at the clock. Three o'clock. Dark. Silent. Perhaps she had been dreaming? Couldn't remember. Didn't want to. Didn't want to think at all.

Kirsty slid her arm down, relaxing against the pillow, unsure whether to wish the night away, or hope the morning would never come. Was there no light at all at the end of the tunnel?

At first the sound of the telephone washed over her, swamped by her feeling of helpless despair. When she did recognise the sound, she hardly dared to answer the summons. Surely no good news would come in the middle of the night?

Unconsciously, she twisted the blue ribbon of her nightdress round her hand, gripping hard as she took up the telephone in shaking fingers.

"Kirsty Trensham."

"I shall pick you up in five minutes. You will be ready, please. I cannot leave the child for long."

"Pick me up to go where?"

"I am bringing you home." He sounded tired. Desperately tired.

"Leif," she spoke gently, "it's three in

318

the morning, and I am home already."

"I know the time. Sorry. But I must bring you to Tall Trees. You are needed here."

"Needed?" She closed her eyes, afraid to believe the implication of his words. "So desperately — in the middle of the night?"

"I know the things I said to you are untrue. I know I should not ask, but Kirsty, we cannot . . . I cannot . . . " His voice broke. "Help me."

Suddenly, she was standing upright, gripping the telephone, speaking earnestly into the mouthpiece.

"Don't leave her, Leif. I'll come to you. I'll be there in five minutes — less — I'll just throw on a coat, and come as I am. All right?"

Kirsty was as good as her word. Within five minutes, she was pulling into the courtyard, running up the steps and into the house.

Closing the door, she turned to find Leif coming down the staircase.

"Where is she?"

"In my bed. The doctor tells me it will help her to rest, but . . . " He gave a weary shrug, and led the way upstairs.

Fear gripped Kirsty's heart as they made the ascent. Why was there no sound of Minna crying, no tearful voice calling Leif's name?

It was only when Leif pushed open the door, and she crossed the room to stand by the bed, looking down on the child, that she realised the explanation. The little girl was too exhausted to cry properly.

"Now then, now then, what's all this?" Gently, Kirsty stroked back the wisps of damp hair from the child's face, and brushed a soft kiss on the wet cheek.

As she leaned closer, Minna held up her arms, and Kirsty laughed softly.

"All right, then. I'll pick you up for a cuddle."

Sitting down on the bed, she lifted the little girl on to her knee. Leif took up the eiderdown, wrapping it round them both and, looking into his face at close quarters, she could see that he, too, was on the point of collapse.

"Why don't you go and get some sleep, Leif?" she suggested gently.

At once, Minna sat bolt upright,

snatching at Leif's hand.

Leif shrugged. "It seems that she wants me to be here, also."

Kirsty nodded. "Of course, she does. I left her, but you didn't. She trusts you. However . . . " she looked down at the child in her arms — "the fact remains that Farbror Leif needs rest, and he isn't going to get it by standing up all night. Suppose you cuddle up together in his bed and have a nice sleep? I won't go away."

Leif lifted the covers for Kirsty to lay the child back in his bed.

"There you are, precious. In you pop." Carefully, Kirsty drew the eiderdown away.

"I'm cold, now," Minna wailed, holding up her arms.

Leif slipped into bed beside her. "Cuddle up to me, and you'll soon be warm."

For a moment he held the child in silence. Then he said softly, "Kirsty will be uncomfortable in the chair, little one. Would you like to lend her your bed for the night?"

"No!" Minna struggled up, out of

Leif's arms. "I want Kirsty to stay here with us, in this big bed. I can move up." The little girl pulled back the covers. "Come on, Kirsty."

As Kirsty hesitated, the little face puckered again. There was nothing else for it. There was obviously plenty of room, and the object of her being here was to keep the child happy.

Avoiding Leif's eyes, Kirsty slipped off her coat and slid into bed, beside Minna. "All right, now?"

Minna nodded. "Mm. That's lovely."

Kirsty gave a relieved sigh. "Then let's see if we can all get some sleep."

Minna snuggled down, and Kirsty relaxed, listening to the deep, regular breathing of the man and the child beside her. How desperate Leif must have been to call her, like this, in the middle of the night, especially when . . .

"Farbror Leif." In her sleep, Minna whimpered.

Kirsty put out a gentle hand to caress the little girl's arm.

The child quietened. Kirsty's eyelids drooped. Sleep. That was what they all needed so badly. In the morning they could talk.

Her hand still touching Minna's arm, Kirsty's mind wandered. Gradually, she drifted into a deep, exhausted sleep.

"Kirsty! Farbror Leif!"

At the sound of the child's voice, two pairs of eyelids stirred, and lifted.

Hazel eyes blinked into equally dazed and uncomprehending blue ones, as both Leif and Kirsty lay perfectly still, unable at first to grasp the fact that they were waking up clasped in each other's arms.

With the realisation that the child was no longer between them, came confusion and embarrassment. Faces flushed, they moved apart, looking anywhere but at each other as they scrambled from each side of the bed and moved to the window, where the child stood pointing.

"Minna Fennel! Whatever are you doing there?"

Struggling to appear relaxed, Kirsty took a shawl from the chair, and placed it round the little girl's shoulders.

"I'm watching this pretty bird."

Kirsty smiled. "I can see that you feel better this morning, but it's a bit too chilly yet to stand there watching it."

She looked round for Leif's approval, only to find that he was across the room, turning back the bedcovers, allowing her to take charge. Well, if that was what he wanted. She turned back to Minna.

"Your window faces the same way, doesn't it? Why not watch it from there — then you can sit in bed and keep warm?"

She lifted the little girl up and moved swiftly across the floor, carrying her through to her own room. The child's bed was by the window.

"There." Kirsty pulled back the covers. "You can still see your pretty bird, and you won't catch cold."

"What's that in your hair, Kirsty?"

As she tucked in the bedclothes, Minna reached to the top of her head. "Oh, it's a little paper horseshoe."

Kirsty laughed. "Confetti. Shows how well I brushed my hair last night."

"What's fetti?" Minna smoothed the horseshoe on her hand.

"Confetti," Kirsty explained, "is the name for the bits of pretty coloured paper that we throw at the bride and groom. I was a guest at my friend Sarah's wedding yesterday."

"Did she have a lovely white dress?" Minna's blue eyes were fixed on her face.

Kirsty nodded. "She certainly did. A beautiful dress of white satin, stitched with tiny pearls."

"Did your friend marry a rich, handsome prince?"

Kirsty laughed. "Well, the first of the three, anyway."

"When I'm grown up," Minna announced, "I'm going to have a wedding like that."

"I hope not," Kirsty sighed. "I hope there's a lot more to your wedding than there was to this one."

"Why?" The little girl was almost pouting.

Kirsty smiled. "Because the wedding itself is only the beginning, love. Like a big party when one of the guests is not going home." She sat down on the edge of the bed. "Think of all your friends, and imagine being with one of them every day for the rest of your life. You'd have to think very carefully about it, and like them very much, wouldn't you? For the bride and groom, you see, the wedding marks the start of a lifetime together. If they don't like each other enough, no pretty dress or mountains of food and flowers will alter the fact."

★ ★ ★

Minna blew on the paper horseshoe, and it floated by the window. "Oh look, Kirsty, there it is again."

She pointed outside just as the bird took flight. "Look at its pretty red wings. What is it?"

Kirsty shook her head. "I don't know. It must be a visitor, I think. I've never seen one of those before."

"It sounds like what Harry calls a Redwing. If so, it comes from Norway."

At the unexpected sound of Leif's voice, Kirsty and Minna jumped and turned, to find him leaning in the doorway, fastening the cuffs of his shirt.

"Look, Farbror Leif . . . " Minna held out her hand . . . "Kirsty had this in her hair."

He came forward, smiling, his wet

hair sparkling in the light from the window. "Perhaps it clings to her for good luck?"

Kirsty smiled. "Perhaps it clings to me because I was too tired to brush my hair properly."

"You have a long journey, ja?"

"Yes," she sighed, "but it wasn't so much the journey. It was the first wedding I've been to, and it was awful . . . just awful . . . and it was Sarah." She gave her head a little shake. "I can't explain."

"I think you have."

Surprised at his reply, Kirsty looked up to encounter such sympathy in his eyes that she knew he understood perfectly.

"Where's Winter?" Minna asked suddenly.

Reluctantly, Kirsty tore her eyes away to look back at the child. "He was in bed with you. Let me see."

She put her hand under the bedclothes, and pulled out the flattened teddy bear. "No wonder he's blue. He hasn't been able to breathe under there. I think you'd better lie down and cuddle him, while I attempt to make myself more

327

respectable." She ran her fingers through her long hair. "You had me so worried that I rushed here without even a hairbrush."

Leif smiled. "I think perhaps I can supply that."

He led the way back to his room and, from a drawer in the dressing-table, produced a beautiful hairbrush, backed with silver and mother-of-pearl. A woman's brush.

Kirsty hesitated as he held it out. "Whose is it?"

Leif gave a wry smile. "Is not Leila's. She has not managed to progress so far into my house."

Still Kirsty made no attempt to take it. He gave his head a little shake.

"Now you are thinking that it belongs to another. It's . . . was . . . my sister Brunhilde's." He offered it again. "Take it, please."

Kirsty took a step back. "Oh no, I couldn't."

He looked sad. "I'm sorry. It offends you because my sister is dead."

"Oh no." Kirsty quickly stepped forward to explain. "It isn't that, at all. It's just that I daren't use anything that is so precious to you."

His eyes were intensely blue. "It's stupid to keep it shut away. Brunhilde was like you: full of life and laughter. She would like you to use it, I am sure."

This time Kirsty took it from him. "Thank you." She spoke softly, beginning to brush the tangles from her hair with long even strokes.

For a moment he stood in silence, watching her, then he moved away to close the drawer. "You would like to have a shower?"

Kirsty stopped brushing. "What bliss. I think that's the thing I miss most of all." She looked down at herself. "Of course, I've nothing here to change into, but the opportunity is too good to miss."

He opened the door to the en suite bathroom, reaching fresh towels from the warming cabinet, giving a cursory glance round. "I think you should find everything you need."

Kirsty blinked. "You mean I can use your shower?"

On the previous occasion, she had used the bathroom leading from the passage.

"You are free to use anything that I have, Kirsty."

It came out as a statement, yet his eyes held a question.

Unsure how she should answer, Kirsty gave him a warm smile as she took the towels from him. "I won't be long." Her smile broadened. "Can't be — I've two goats waiting to be milked."

Leif returned the smile. "If you'd like to give me your key, I'll collect some clothes for you, and tend to your stock."

"Are you sure?"

He nodded. "If you leave now, Minna will think you're not coming back."

Kirsty turned quickly, to hide her disappointment. Clearly his need of her was only in connection with his inability to cope with the child alone.

She fished the key from her coat pocket. "Would you like me to start preparing breakfast, if I'm ready before you are back?"

He smiled again. "If it is no trouble — and Minna will allow you long enough out of her sight."

★ ★ ★

Peeping in on Minna, after tearing herself away from the luxury of the shower, Kirsty found the little girl fast asleep. It was an ideal opportunity to slip down to the kitchen.

She was at the bottom of the stairs when the hall telephone rang. Pouncing on it, to prevent the sound waking Minna, she was surprised to find Mr. Fawcett on the other end of the line.

"Ah, Miss . . . er . . . Kirsty. Just the person. Robert Fawcett here."

Kirsty frowned. "You wanted me, Mr. Fawcett?"

"You and Mr. Amundsen, both," the solicitor qualified. "I just wanted to let you know that the documents re the purchase of Westfield Farm are prepared, and ready for signature. Would ten o'clock tomorrow suit you?"

"Oh, I see," Kirsty hesitated. "Mr. Amundsen isn't here right now, so I can't say for sure. I'll give him your message, Mr. Fawcett, and unless you hear to the contrary you can take it that the ten o'clock appointment suits him.

331

Will that be all right?"

"Fine, Kirsty — and you will be able to make that time, I take it?"

"Me?" Kirsty said. "I'm afraid you're mistaken, Mr. Fawcett. The purchase of Westfield has nothing to do with me at all."

"It certainly has, you know." The solicitor sounded amused. "Mr. Amundsen asked me to prepare documents for a joint purchase, between Miss Kirsty Trensham and himself. His instructions were most explicit, my dear, and the documents will require your signature, along with his."

Puzzling over the startling revelation, Kirsty was automatically measuring coffee into the percolator when she heard the front door open and close.

"You're back quickly." She turned from the dresser as the kitchen door opened. "I expected I would have . . . "

She stopped, appalled. The person facing her with a hostile glare was not Leif — it was Leila Fennel.

"So that's the way of it?" Leila eyed Kirsty's flimsy apparel.

Kirsty said nothing and, after a moment, Leila sneered. "You needn't think that having an affair will help you to become permanent mistress of Tall Trees. I intend to hold that position, and nothing is going to get in my way."

Placing the brown sugar on the tray, Kirsty regarded her steadily. "Don't you think it's Leif's place to choose who he wants?"

"Leif doesn't know what he wants," said Leila in disgust.

"And you don't care?" Spoon in hand, Kirsty remained still.

Leila shrugged. "A man is measured by his material wealth."

Kirsty shook her head. "Not in my opinion. It seems to me that you would like to be the honoured mistress of Tall Trees, regardless of what happened to the master; whereas I would deem it an honour to be Leif Amundsen's wife, regardless of his position in life."

Leila remained silent, and turning back to the tray, Kirsty laughed.

"There's little point in our arguing, anyway. I expect neither of us will get our wish. I think it highly unlikely that Leif will want me around for the remainder of his days, and I pray that he doesn't choose to have you, Miss Fennel. If he does, I have little doubt that both he and the child will be thoroughly miserable in a very short time — and you won't even care."

She replaced the sugar canister on the shelf and, when she turned back again, Leila had gone.

She sighed. Now she'd upset her again. She was bound to meet Leif on the way back, and present the conversation in entirely the opposite way to the truth. What would he . . . ?

Her thoughts were interrupted by something fluttering at the window. A butterfly was moving up and down the pane. As Kirsty approached, it came to rest, the beautifully marked wings gently raising and lowering.

"A Red Admiral, no less." Kirsty smiled, carefully opening the window. "There, off you go to sail about in the sunshine."

The butterfly remained still. "Come on, now. Action stations." Kirsty put out a gentle finger. "Move right a bit — I mean port, of course, or is it starboard?"

She laughed as the creature moved sideways to perch on her finger.

"Very nice, I'm sure, but I can't make breakfast with you on there. Anyway, it's much better outside."

The butterfly fluttered once, then took off and was soon out of sight. "There you go. Eat up all my nettles, there's a good chap." She closed the window. "Now, where was I?"

"Making the coffee, I think."

She jumped violently as Leif's voice came from just across the room. He was leaning against the edge of the table, arms folded, crossed legs outstretched to their full length.

Kirsty's lips parted. "How long have you been there?"

He grinned. "I come in as Leila goes out." He nodded towards the window. "It's starboard — see, I know your language better than you do."

She made a face. "Big-headed foreigner!"

"In my country you will be the foreigner."

Kirsty shrugged. "If I ever get to your country — which is extremely doubtful, I feel."

"Not at all. It's necessary that you do."

As the blue eyes raked her face, Kirsty frowned. "Necessary?"

He gave a slight nod. "If you are to be *min kone* you will need to meet the family."

She swallowed visibly. "You came in before Leila went out. You heard every word, didn't you?"

Leif's eyes twinkled. "I cannot tell a lie."

"And I suppose it would be no good trying to convince you that I wasn't serious?"

He gave his head a slow, deliberate shake.

"I suppose you know that I feel a complete fool?"

"Because you love me, or because I know about it?"

She flushed. "Because you know about it."

For a moment longer, her gaze remained centred on the tray, then suddenly she lifted one of the mugs, and replaced it on the dresser.

"Where are my clothes?"

He half-turned, indicating the pile on the chair, by the door.

"Thank you. I think it's time I was going home."

"And I think is time you learned when I am teasing, and came over here to kiss me."

She shook her head. "Leif, you don't have to . . . "

He clicked his tongue. "Has it never occurred to you, Kirsty, that I might feel the same way about you?"

★ ★ ★

Unable for the moment to believe her ears, Kirsty raised her head slowly to find the blue eyes so full of longing, that she was unable to tear her own away.

Suddenly, he smiled. "You cannot wish to be *min kone* any more than I have longed for it myself." He held out his arms. "Come to me, Kirsty, please."

He caught her as she ran to him, cradling her against his chest, kissing the tears from her face, as she sobbed. "I thought I had lost you. Oh Leif, I thought I would never see you again."

"Is this what I have done to my little Miss Sunshine?"

She raised her head, blinking the tears away. "Miss Sunshine?"

He smiled. "Ja. Is my name for you. Every day, when I am getting up, I think: I wonder if my Miss Sunshine is awake, and how she is planning to spend her day. I wish she is spending it with me."

Kirsty brushed soft lips against his cheek. "It's a lovely name. Why did you think I might not like it?"

He shrugged. "At the time, I think you do not like me to think of you as belonging to me. If I had known then . . . "

Kirsty looked deep into the blue eyes. "If we had both known then, darling."

His smile faded. "You have called me several names in the past, but this I like best of all."

She stroked soft fingers down the back of his neck. "It's the first time I have said it, but it's how I have thought of you for a long time."

He closed his eyes momentarily, then

opened them again, his breathing suddenly quickened. Lifting her from her feet, he shouldered his way out of the room and into the lounge, laying her gently down on the soft red velvet cushions, kneeling beside her.

As his lips possessed hers, she pressed closer, clinging to him. Wanting nothing except to belong to him completely, knowing or caring nothing beyond his gentle, stroking hands, and the circle of her lover's arms.

"Farbror . . . Kirsty. Where are you?"

With a sigh, Leif buried his face for a moment, against her neck. "The joys of fatherhood."

Hugging him close, Kirsty laughed. "Tell me something. Why are you Farbror Leif, when the Norwegian word for uncle is 'onkel' — it's very misleading when the word sounds so much like 'father'?"

He grinned. "Is not my fault that the Swedish people use a similar word."

Kirsty frowned. "Swedish? But you told me that you were Norwegian."

He laughed. "My mother is Swedish, and it is she who teaches the little one. The languages are very alike, yet some words very different. Minna found 'onkel' difficult to say, but could manage my mother's word 'farbror' . . . So . . . " He shrugged. "I am Farbror Leif."

He was suddenly serious, looking deep into her eyes.

"At first, when I am told of the accident, I cannot believe it. Suddenly, Brunhilde is dead, my good friend Robin in intensive care — unable to be moved — and there is a tiny child waiting for collection at the hospital. I did not want to go there, did not want to see her, but I had no choice."

His expression softened, and he gave a little smile, remembering. "When, at last, I look down on the child, she is so small and helpless that I cannot help loving her. I am glad when it is decided to keep her here at Tall Trees: at the time we are hoping that to see his daughter will help Robin recover, but he did not regain sufficient understanding. The day after the accident, Robbie comes from Norway to help me, and somehow we cope. But it has not been easy."

As he stopped speaking, he hugged her close, burying his face for a moment against her soft hair.

Kirsty tightened her arms about him. "It will be easier from now on, my darling, I promise."

As they breakfasted in Minna's room, Kirsty remembered the telephone call. Quickly, she explained Mr. Fawcett's message.

"He seemed to think it was a joint purchase, but I told him he was mistaken."

Leif shook his head, laughing. "You are the one to be mistaken, my darling. You think that I allow you to look after my house for nothing? I know that if I offer you money you will not take it, so I put it to good purpose."

He gripped her shoulders, looking earnestly down into her face.

"It's ours, Kirsty — just as everything else will be ours, very soon." He smiled, loosening his hold. "The way I feel at this moment, the sooner the better, I think. We must spend the day making arrangements."

"Arrangements?"

Leif's eyes twinkled. "For the wedding." He slid his arms back round her waist,

341

crossing his wrists behind her. He was grinning. "We must have a wedding for you to be mother to my sons."

Kirsty's eyes widened. "And who said we are going to have sons?"

"I say so." Leif straightened to his full height, assuming an attitude of arrogance. "A Viking expects his woman to obey."

She tossed her head. "Oh, he does, does he?"

Kirsty grinned down at Minna. "Bossy like this with you, is he, this uncle of yours?"

Minna giggled, and Kirsty turned back to Leif. "You win. What do you do first when fixing a wedding?"

"Make a list." From Minna's desk, he took up paper and pencil, marking out two columns. "One for you and one for me," he explained. "Yours first. Who do you wish to invite to our wedding?"

"Can Timothy come, Leif?" Her question was so prompt, that he laughed.

"If he had not been on your list, he would have been on mine."

She smiled. "Thank you."

He wrote the name with a flourish. "So Master Timothy is at the top of the list."

Kirsty sighed. "Correction. He is the list."

Pencil in mid-air, his eyes swept her face. "There is no one else?"

She shook her head. "No relatives. Friends here should go on your list, rather than mine. There would have been Sarah, but . . . "

Leaning forward, he took her small hands into his huge ones.

"You have a list of one, and I have millions. It's going to be so different for you to belong to such a large family. I hope you do not find it too exhausting when we go to visit."

She smiled. "I shall love every minute of it. I always wanted a family. I only wish we could be married among them."

His grip tightened. "You would like to be married in Norway?"

She blinked at his suddenly tense expression. "I know it's not practical, of course. It's just that weddings are a family time, and since I don't have one . . . "

To her surprise he gave a delighted laugh. "It's a marvellous idea. My mother will be so pleased."

He sat forward, his face alive with anticipation. "In our village it's customary to wear National costume at weddings. There is a set passed down from my great-grandmother. It's worn by my grandmother, my mother, and Brunhilde."

"Hey! Just a minute. Hold your horses." Kirsty broke into his volume of words. "Heirlooms like that are for the use of the daughters of the household — the direct line. Minna will come into that category, but not me. I am not only an outsider. I am also English, remember?"

Leif shook his head, his eyes twinkling. "It's passed on by my paternal grand-mother — who has no daughters. So my mother is in the same position as you."

"But she is Norwegian," Kirsty insisted.

Again he shook his head. "Swedish!" he reminded her.

★ ★ ★

The beauty of the tree-lined fjord took Kirsty's breath away, as she walked with Leif at the head of the bridal procession,

344

on their way from the small Lutheran church.

The black embroidered skirt, red vest and white blouse, had been lovingly tucked and stitched by Leif's mother until it fitted to perfection, and with the traditional gilt crown on her head, she presented as lovely a bride as the friendly village people ever remembered.

At the time, feeling the object of attention of hundreds of eyes, she clutched at her new husband's hand nervously, in complete awe of the situation.

Afterwards, it was the amusing things that she remembered.

Jenny, leaving in the midst of the festivities to inspect a villager's goat — the only word, in each other's language, that either could understand; Timothy, in a quiet corner, with a bag of marbles and all the professionalism of a river-boat hustler, extorting the most-prized possession — a lizard skeleton — from a Norwegian counterpart.

Hours later, gazing from the windows of the huge timber building that Leif had described as a forest hut, Kirsty could scarcely believe her eyes.

"It's vast." Turning wondering eyes to Leif as he came up behind her, she smiled. "I can't believe it's all yours."

"Ours, Kirsty," he corrected.

She shook her head. "It will always be yours, to me."

Leif nodded. "As it will always be my grandfather's to me." He laughed suddenly, winding his arms about her. "Now you know why I need the sons: they work, and their father stays at home with their mother."

Kirsty laughed. "Got it all worked out, haven't you?"

"From this moment on," he assured her.

"And what, then, have you planned for the next hour or so?"

He tightened his hold, pulling her back against him, bending his head, to whisper in her ear. "You cannot guess?"